PL

The only [...] t the
Dairi Burger [...] essica
was A. J. Morgan. And every time she looked
at him she felt a surge of conflicting emotions: panic, confusion, frustration, and head-
over-heels love. She couldn't do anything to
jeopardize the good opinion he had of her.
He liked the quiet, concerned type, so she
had to *be* the quiet, concerned type.

"You're looking pretty serious." A. J.'s voice
broke gently into her reverie. He was smiling
at her in a way that made her heart race.

She blushed. "Oh, I was thinking about—
about nuclear war," she fibbed lamely. "You
know—how terrible it would be if there was
one and everything."

The smile vanished from his face. Nodding
slowly, he picked up his soda, then took a
long swallow. "You're right," he agreed softly,
his eyes clouding over.

As Jessica turned to talk to Lila, she felt a
twinge of anxiety. Hadn't A. J. looked surprised, maybe even confused?

She hoped she hadn't said something wrong.
Or stupid. She didn't want to do anything
that would ruin her chances with A.J. He
was too important to her.

Bantam Books in the Sweet Valley High series
Ask your bookseller for the books you have missed

SWEET VALLEY HIGH

PLAYING
FOR KEEPS

Written by
Kate William

Created by
FRANCINE PASCAL

BANTAM BOOKS
TORONTO · NEW YORK · LONDON · SYDNEY · AUCKLAND

PLAYING FOR KEEPS

A Bantam Book / October 1988

Sweet Valley High is a registered trademark of Francine Pascal.

Conceived by Francine Pascal.

Produced by Daniel Weiss Associates, Inc.,
27 West 20th Street,
New York, NY 10011

Cover art by James Mathewuse.

ISBN 0-553-27477-5

Published simultaneously in the United States and Canada

Bantam Books are published by Bantam Books, a division of Bantam Doubleday Dell Publishing Group, Inc. Its trademark, consisting of the words "Bantam Books" and the portrayal of a rooster, is Registered in U.S. Patent and Trademark Office and in other countries. Marca Registrada. Bantam Books, 666 Fifth Avenue, New York, New York 10103.

PRINTED IN THE UNITED STATES OF AMERICA

O   0 9 8 7 6 5 4 3 2 1

PLAYING FOR KEEPS

One

Elizabeth Wakefield wrapped her arms around her knees and let out a blissful sigh. A few yards away from her, the gentle waves of the Pacific Ocean lapped at the sand, leaving a line of foam along the beach as they receded. It was a sunny Friday afternoon, and a big crowd from Sweet Valley High had gathered at their favorite spot on the beach.

She watched her boyfriend, Jeffrey French, surface from a wave and shake the water from his blond hair. Sending her a gleaming smile, he strode toward her through the knee-deep water.

"Boy, was I dumb," Elizabeth said to her best friend, Enid Rollins, who was sitting next to her on the beach blanket.

Enid looked up from her book and raised an eyebrow. "Huh?"

"You know—that slam book mess. I can't believe I took it so seriously when Jeffrey's name kept appearing with Olivia's. I really acted like a dope."

Enid rolled her green eyes and shook her head, and Elizabeth turned to Jeffrey just as he sat down at her other side.

While he toweled himself off, Elizabeth studied him from under her lashes. For the last few weeks, Sweet Valley High had been in the grip of slam book fever. Nearly every girl at school had the same marbleized-cover notebook. Each page was headed by a category, such as Class Clown, Biggest Flirt, or Biggest Jock. There was even a section for predictions called the Crystal Ball. When the books were passed around, girls entered their choices anonymously. At first Elizabeth thought it was just a lot of harmless fun.

But then people began writing Jeffrey's name under Couples of the Future—with Olivia Davidson's. The first few times she saw it, Elizabeth shrugged it off. Olivia was a pretty good friend of hers, and besides, Olivia had been dating Roger Patman steadily for several months.

Soon things got out of control, especially when Elizabeth's name began to appear in the same Couples of the Future category with a new junior from Atlanta named A. J. Morgan. No matter who tried making excuses and explanations, tempers flared up, and feelings were hurt. Fortunately, though, Elizabeth and Jeffrey sorted out the groundless rumors before disaster struck.

As though sensing her intense scrutiny, Jeffrey looked up and met her eyes, and Elizabeth felt a surge of emotion. They had worked out their problems and resolved their differences, and now she and Jeffrey were as much in love as ever.

"Hey, Most Popular," he teased, referring to one of the slam book categories in which Elizabeth's name had appeared frequently.

She grinned and stuck out her tongue. "Only tied for first place, don't forget."

"Well, I don't know if that really counts," Enid said. "I mean, two people who look exactly alike and talk alike and everything else—that's not really sharing first place. You're most popular as a *unit*."

Jeffrey laughed. "Hey, that's true," he agreed.

Suppressing a grin, Elizabeth shot a look over her shoulder at a nearby trio of girls. Sitting between her two best friends was Elizabeth's identical twin sister, Jessica. Only the people who knew them well could tell them apart at a glance. They had the same sun-streaked blond hair, the same twinkling blue-green eyes, and the same beautiful heart-shaped faces. Each of them had a perfect size-six figure: five feet six inches of California girl. Growing up in the perpetual sunshine of Sweet Valley had given them a healthy glow that anyone would envy. Right down to the dimples in their left cheeks, Elizabeth and Jessica were mirror images of each other.

But the similarity stopped there, as everyone who met them discovered after approximately seven seconds! The older twin by four minutes, Elizabeth was more mature and practical than her headstrong sister. She liked books and music, writing poetry, and sharing ideas and dreams with her closest friends, Jeffrey and Enid. One of her dreams was to be a professional writer, and she was practicing by writing articles and a weekly column for *The Oracle*, Sweet Valley High's school newspaper. She had a reputation for being dependable, honest, and fair-minded, and everyone at Sweet Valley liked and admired her for that.

Of course, nearly everyone at Sweet Valley liked and admired Jessica, too, but for completely different reasons. Her attitude toward life was positively regal. She liked to believe that everything revolved around her. She was willful and impetuous and constantly got herself into scrapes and predicaments by acting first, then thinking about the consequences later. Frequently her escapades caused her to teeter on the brink of disaster, but someone always bailed her out. More often than not it was her reliable twin who came to her rescue. Jessica breezed through life with a nonchalant confidence that most people couldn't help being impressed by.

So it was no surprise that the Wakefield twins had tied for Most Popular. Between them they represented every exciting and lovable quality a sixteen-year-old could have.

"Speaking of slam books, there's our future high school coach," Enid said with a giggle, arching her eyebrows significantly as she looked toward Ken Matthews.

The tall blond football star was organizing a game of volleyball. Ken's name had appeared in the Crystal Ball section of the slam books under Most Likely to Be a High School Coach, and everyone agreed it was one of the most perfect choices.

Elizabeth grinned. "Can't you just see him? Maybe we should get him a whistle."

"And then we have the Girl with the Most of Everything, and Most Likely to Appear on the Cover of *Time*," Enid went on in a singsong tone, pointing with her chin toward wealthy

Lila Fowler and ambitious Amy Sutton, two of Jessica's good friends. "And don't forget—"

"Biggest Flirt," Elizabeth cut in with a laugh. She looked back affectionately at her twin. That was Jessica Wakefield all the way.

"So then he goes, 'You look *so* hot, Amy. We should get together sometime.'" Amy Sutton smiled archly as she rubbed suntan lotion on her arms.

Jessica caught Lila Fowler's gaze and crossed her eyes. Instantly Lila sputtered with laughter and buried her face in a towel.

"What?" Amy demanded indignantly. Her gray eyes narrowed as she frowned at Jessica. "What did you say?"

"Nothing. I didn't say anything, did I, Li?" Angelic and innocent as a baby, Jessica shook her head and shrugged. "Honest. Go on. So then what did he say, Amy?"

Still suspicious, Amy continued her monologue about the "gorgeous hunk" she had met at the Beach Disco the night before. Jessica kept her interested smile plastered on her face, but secretly she was bored. There was really only one person whose life kept her constantly fascinated, and that was her own. Of course, Amy was a good friend, but sometimes she droned on much too long.

"So did he ask for your phone number or what?" Lila interrupted.

Shrugging nonchalantly, Amy shook her head. "No, but I gave it to him anyway."

Jessica snorted, then opened her mouth to make one of her typically snide retorts. But as she raised her head, her eyes became fixed on the tall, redheaded boy striding across the beach in her direction. She snapped her mouth shut, feeling a blush color her cheeks. It was A. J. Morgan.

Before A.J. had appeared on the scene, Jessica's habit had always been to flit from one boy to another. A full-time commitment, like the one her twin had with Jeffrey, had never made any sense to her. After all, why be stuck with just one boy when she could go out with so many? She had had her share of serious crushes, too. But luckily they never lasted very long!

But when A. J. Morgan came to Sweet Valley High, Jessica knew she was in love from the first time she saw him. Really in love. This wasn't just an infatuation, physical attraction, or her usual crush. This was the real thing. And A.J. seemed to like Jessica, too. There was just one hitch, though: the Jessica he liked was one who acted more like Elizabeth than Jessica.

It was such a stupid, idiotic mix-up. Just being around A.J. had thrown Jessica into such an emotional tailspin that she had been quiet and reserved, rather than vivacious and outgoing.

And then, in addition to Jessica's personality switch, Elizabeth had suddenly changed into a Jessica clone. Because of the rumors about Jeffrey and Olivia in the slam books, Elizabeth had decided to come on super-strong and seductive toward A.J.—whom she didn't know her sister liked—in order to make Jeffrey jealous. When that happened, A.J. was more than a little taken aback. He had even confessed that that kind of hurricane approach—Jessica's *usual* approach— was too overwhelming for him! So he came to the conclusion that Jessica, being the quieter, more easygoing twin, was the one he liked better! It was all totally backward.

Under any other circumstances Jessica would have straightened him out in two seconds. But the thought that he wouldn't care about her anymore if he knew what she was really like was enough to make her heart stop beating completely.

What am I going to do? she asked herself frantically. *I don't want to lose him!*

For the time being, all she *could* do was keep up the act. She had to keep playing it quiet and serious, sweet and sincere. She sent up a silent vote of thanks for having decided to wear a conservative blue tank suit to the beach instead of one of her sexy string bikinis. She scrambled to her feet as A.J. approached, then waited in tongue-tied silence for him to speak first.

"Hi, Jessica," he called out, his red hair falling into his eyes.

Her fingers itched to brush his hair away, but she didn't dare do anything so brash and personal. Instead, she gave him a sweet, demure smile and then dropped her eyes. "Hi, A.J.," she breathed. Her heart raced just having him near her.

From one corner of her eye, she saw Lila and Amy looking at her with undisguised skepticism. Giving a mental shrug, she moved away from her friends and smiled again at A.J. He followed her willingly.

"So, how's it going?" He sat down to empty sand from his worn boat shoes and nodded invitingly toward the space next to him.

Her heart fluttering, Jessica sank down beside him and stared out across the gently lapping waves. She couldn't think of a thing to say, something that had never happened to her before she met A.J.

"I thought you might be here," he began as he leaned back and propped himself up on one elbow. He grinned at her, and his warm brown eyes sparkled as he squinted against the glare.

"Oh, I-I'm always at the beach," Jessica stammered. "I just love being outside—and—and the fresh air and everything." That was the kind of Girl Scout attitude he was attracted to, she thought. And she prayed she could keep up her act convincingly.

"Yeah, me, too."

Her mind raced as she desperately tried to think of what her twin would talk about. She drew a deep breath. "Isn't it amazing how those same waves came all the way from Japan? Or is it China? Or—I mean, it makes you realize how close but—but how far away, I mean . . ." She let her words trail off, unsure of exactly what she was trying to say. In agony she gave him a hopeful smile.

He looked thoughtful. "Yeah, I guess I know what you mean. I guess that means surfers are kind of like diplomats, right?" he teased.

Letting out a peal of polite laughter, Jessica shook her head. "I don't know about that."

A.J. breathed a contented sigh as he leaned his head back, eyes closed, to soak up the sunshine. It took all of Jessica's self-control not to turn on her full seductive power and simply pounce. But if she did, she was afraid he'd bolt like a racehorse. Instead, she quickly looked away and tucked her knees up to her chin. She swore she was going to make this relationship work, even if she had to turn her whole personality inside out to guarantee it.

Lila rolled over on her stomach and rested her chin on her fists. Jessica and A.J. were in her line of sight, and she knew her friend well enough to realize that something very peculiar was going on. Every movement Jessica made seemed out of character. She usually had no trouble showing off her perfect figure once she was at the beach. Now there she was, sitting all curled up in a tight little ball. It didn't make any sense, Lila thought. Jessica had told her that she was crazy about A.J.

"Have you noticed how bizarre Jessica has been acting lately?" Lila asked, her brown eyes narrowed suspiciously.

Amy flipped through a few more glossy pages of *Ingenue* before she answered. "Well, now that you mention it, I guess you're right. But only when *he*'s around, it seems," she pointed out, nodding her head toward A.J. "Wow, look at this *dress*."

"Let me see." Impatiently Lila reached for the magazine, ran her eyes over the low-cut, clingy dress, and tossed it back. "Yeah, that's a

Nadine original. They have it at Lisette's. I'm thinking of buying it. But listen, Amy, I'm serious."

Amy assumed an intent, listening expression. "OK, Lila. You're serious."

"I mean it," Lila insisted, scowling. She turned her eyes back to Jessica and A.J. and shook her head. "I think we should say something to her. She's acting like a completely different person."

"Hmmm . . ." Amy's mocking look faded as she followed Lila's gaze. "Actually, that's probably a good idea. 'Cause if this is some weird way of getting A.J. I have a feeling it isn't going to work."

Two

"A.J.?"

"Mmm?"

He looked at her with a sleepy smile that made Jessica melt inside.

"I was thinking," she continued, digging her fingers into the sand and trying to sound earnest. "I know it's a really nice day, but maybe we could go to the library. I need to get my homework done, and that really has to come first. Do you want to go with me?"

A slightly surprised look came into A.J.'s gold-flecked eyes. But he shrugged good-naturedly and gave her a grin. "Sure. I guess so, Jessica. If that's what you want to do, that's OK with me."

"Oh, great," she breathed. A feeling of relief flooded through her. It had been a smart move after all, it seemed. He couldn't help being impressed by her dedication and sense of purpose. After pulling on her shorts and shirt, scooping up her things, and saying goodbye to her friends, she walked with A.J. toward his car, talking soberly the whole way.

"I have a report to do for English, and I really want it to be good," she explained, an intent expression on her face. "I mean, I know a lot of kids our age think grades and stuff don't matter, or that it isn't cool to care, but I know how important they are."

She snuck a look up at his profile, trying to gauge his reaction. One of the most attractive things about A.J. was his vaguely mysterious air. Most of the time he was open and candid, but there were also times when it was impossible to tell what was going through his mind. At the moment she wasn't sure what he was thinking, so she decided just to keep going to play it safe.

"And I know you'll think this sounds weird, but nothing makes me feel better than showing my parents a good report card," she confessed modestly.

As he loped along beside her, A.J. looked at her with a smile of appreciation. "That's amazing, Jessica. Most people just think grades are one big drag."

"Not me," she insisted. Her voice was grave.

They reached his car, and he held the door open as he gave her a gallant little salute. "After you."

She smiled sweetly up into his eyes. "Thank you."

"To the library?" he prompted, a slightly doubtful look on his face.

"To the library," Jessica repeated with a firm nod.

Jessica leaned across the table and whispered throatily, "A.J.? Can I read you something?"

Looking up from his book, A.J. gave her a quick nod and leaned back in his chair. "Sure. What is it?"

"One of my favorite poems," she replied, meeting his eyes with a luminous smile.

It had been one of her favorites since she found it the night before. Poetry wasn't exactly something she dipped into on a regular basis, but serious, sincere people like Elizabeth loved poetry, so Jessica decided she had better like it, too. Besides, she knew A.J. really liked poetry. Just the week before, they had gone to a party to celebrate Sweet Valley High's new literary magazine, and A.J. had been very interested in it. Since it was Jessica's plan to show him how much they had in common, she had scoured Elizabeth's poetry books until she found what she considered the deepest, most soulful poems. They were guaranteed to tell A.J. what she was like on the inside.

While her heart flip-flopped with nervous anticipation, she pulled a slim volume of poetry from her book bag and opened it up to a marked page. Then she cleared her throat and drew a deep breath. "This is a poem by Emily Dickinson," she said.

In a voice throbbing with emotional intensity, she read, " 'If I can stop one Heart from breaking/I shall not live in vain. . . .' "

She read the entire poem with as much drama and intensity as she could muster, then raised her head from the book and sighed. "Isn't it beautiful?" she asked.

A.J. nodded slowly and gave her a gentle smile. "It's really nice," he agreed. He leaned forward suddenly and rested his chin in one hand. "You know, I was thinking—"

"Wait, there's another one," she broke in, hastily flipping through the pages of *One Hundred and One Famous Poems*. "I know you'll like this one—it's so emotional. Can I just read it to you?"

Shrugging, A.J. sat back again. "Sure, Jessica. Go ahead."

16

"This one is by Walt Whitman, and it's called 'O Captain! My Captain!' "

She squared her shoulders, held the book in front of her the way singers did in a choir, and drew a deep breath. Giving it every heartfelt, earnest nuance she could muster, she began to read.

When she paused to draw a breath, she relished the rasping emotional catch she was sure she could hear in her voice.

"Wow, that is intense," A.J. commented, nodding his head appreciatively.

Jessica's face fell. "But that's just the first stanza! There's a whole bunch more—"

"Oh, well . . ." A.J. shifted in his chair. "Maybe I could read it myself sometime. I mean, not that you don't read it well," he assured her hastily. "But it's so hard to get all of a poem just hearing it, you know? At least it is for me," he added with a sheepish grin.

"Oh. I know what you mean. You're right."

Secretly Jessica was a little disappointed that she hadn't been able to read the entire poem, but at least A.J. sounded impressed with her poetic taste. This was obviously the sort of profound, intellectual thing that he responded to. She promised herself she would keep at it, no matter what.

"Jessica?"

A.J. was gazing at her with a hopeful, little-boy look in his eyes. It took all her willpower not to lean across the table and kiss him. Instead, she whispered huskily, "Yes?"

"Would you mind if we left pretty soon? I mean, whenever you're ready, but I was hoping we could go to the Dairi Burger and get something to eat. I'm starved."

"Oh. OK. Sure, whatever you want."

"How about now?" he urged.

Jessica met his warm, twinkling eyes and felt breathless. She still couldn't get over the effect he had on her. Smiling and nodding, she pushed back her chair. "Sure. Let's go."

As he drove, A.J. talked about what it was like being an "army brat," moving around the country every two or three years as his father was reassigned to different posts. Jessica tried to appear sympathetic, but all she could think about was how cute he looked when his hair fell into his eyes and how strong and sensitive his hands seemed as they gripped the steering wheel.

She came back to reality as they pulled into the Dairi Burger parking lot.

"I guess everybody hangs out here pretty much all the time, right?" he asked as they walked up to the front door.

Jessica hesitated before answering. She didn't

want to sound frivolous, but she also didn't want to sound like a total dud. "Well, yeah, I guess so. When I have some spare time after all my work is finished, it's a good place to relax."

The truth was, she was there almost every day. The Dairi Burger was the perfect place to see and keep track of everything that was happening in Sweet Valley. And it was the perfect place to *be* seen, too. But she didn't want A.J. to get the impression she cared about those things.

They stepped inside the noisy burger joint. A huge gang of kids had pulled some tables together and were having a noisy feast. Lila and Amy were there, as were Winston Egbert, Ken Matthews, Bruce Patman, and at least a dozen other juniors and seniors from Sweet Valley High. Jessica was dying to be in the center of the group in her usual starring role, but she knew it wouldn't fit in with her new image. Smiling shyly, she glanced up into A.J.'s face.

"There's a booth free over there," she offered, pointing to the other side of the room.

He grinned. "OK, but how about if we sit with everybody else? We could—"

"Jessica! A.J.! Over here!" Winston's voice roared out across the room, and he stood up on his chair to wave his arms wildly over his head.

Laughing, A.J. shrugged his shoulders. "Looks like we're being drafted, anyway."

"OK," she replied, secretly relieved. "I don't mind." She followed behind as he wove through the crowded tables to the group. There was a chorus of hellos.

"Hey, Jess, where've you been lately, anyway? We're all dying of boredom without you," Winston moaned as she and A.J. found two seats. Winston leaned across the table and gave Jessica a melancholy look. "We miss you."

Stifling a sarcastic retort, Jessica managed a pleasant smile. "Gee, Win, you know I'm not a real party animal," she said sweetly. "I've been busy."

Winston instantly looked intrigued, and he threw a grin across his shoulder at the others. "What do you think, guys? Think this is really Jessica? Or is it Liz?"

Bruce Patman, the wealthiest boy at Sweet Valley High, leaned back in his chair and gave Jessica an appraising glance. He and Jessica had dated for a while, but now there was a cold war between them. "I don't know," Bruce said. "It's hard to tell lately."

"I don't know why you say that," Jessica said tensely. She snuck a quick glance at A.J. and smiled even wider. But the look she shot back at Bruce was pure venom.

Next to her, Lila spoke in a taunting, sarcastic voice pitched low so only Jessica could hear. "How was studying, Jess?" she teased. Her eyes sparkled with mischief, and she shot a knowing look in A.J.'s direction. "Get much work done?"

"Yes, I did," Jessica replied, gritting her teeth behind her smile.

Turning back to A.J., she asked in a soft, lilting tone, "Do you think you could get me a diet Coke?"

He shoved his chair back immediately and rose to his feet with a nod. "Sure. I'll be right back."

Jessica waited until he was safely out of earshot, then whirled around on her best friend. "You can be such a pain, Lila. Why don't you just back off?"

"Why, what do you mean, Jess?" Lila cooed, imitating Jessica's own gentle "Elizabeth" tone. She took a long sip of diet soda through her straw and grinned devilishly at Jessica as she studied her clothes. Taking in the light blue Bermuda shorts and the polo shirt Jessica had borrowed from Elizabeth, she said, "It *is* Jessica, isn't it?"

Fuming, Jessica turned in her chair, and her gaze landed on Winston. "*Don't* say a *word*," she commanded as he opened his mouth. She held up one hand and narrowed her eyes at him. "I'm warning you, Win—"

"Here you go."

A.J. handed her a tall paper cup brimming with soda, and Jessica shut her mouth with a snap. "Thanks."

Across the table Bruce and Winston were both looking at her with impish grins, and she studiously ignored them. While A.J. began a conversation with Maria Santelli, Winston's girlfriend, Jessica concentrated on her soda. She didn't dare look anyone in the face in case she was tempted to shoot out some typical Jessica remark. Inwardly she realized what a dumb situation it was, and she knew she was acting unnatural. Everyone else knew it, too.

And they're all trying to sabotage me, she thought.

The only person in the whole group who didn't know the real Jessica was sitting next to her. And every time she looked at him, glanced up at his profile as he talked with friendly ease to Maria, she felt a surge of conflicting emotions: panic, confusion, frustration, and head-over-heels love. She couldn't do anything to jeopardize the good opinion he had of her. He liked the quiet, concerned type, so she had to *be* the quiet, concerned type.

"You're looking pretty serious." A.J.'s voice

broke gently into her reverie. He was smiling at her in a way that made her heart race.

She blushed. "Oh, I was thinking about—about nuclear war," she fibbed lamely. "You know—how terrible it would be if there were one and everything."

The smile vanished from his face. Nodding slowly, he picked up his soda, then took a long swallow. "You're right," he agreed softly, his eyes clouding over.

As Jessica turned to talk to Lila she felt a twinge of anxiety. Hadn't A.J. looked surprised, maybe even confused?

She hoped she hadn't said something wrong. Or stupid. She didn't want to do anything that would ruin her chances with A.J. He was too important to her.

After school on Monday, Elizabeth swung her book bag over her shoulder and headed for the newspaper office. There were some items for next week's "Eyes and Ears" column she wanted to get on paper while her thoughts were fresh. As she rounded a corner she narrowly missed a head-on collision with A.J.

"Ooops! Sorry about that," she said, laughing and stepping aside.

To her surprise A.J. blushed and shuffled his feet.

"Listen, I'm glad I found you. I wanted to tell you I'll be a few minutes late for the meeting. I have to go to the administration office and straighten out a problem with my transcript, but I'll be there as soon as I can," he said in a breathless rush.

Elizabeth stared at him in perplexed astonishment and shook her head. "What?"

"The Save the Whales meeting. I'm really sorry."

"What Save the Whales meeting? What are you talking about?"

He gave her a puzzled look and dug his hands into his pockets. "Didn't you say you wanted to go to that meeting today, Jessica?"

"Jess—?" Elizabeth laughed. "I'm Liz, A.J."

"Oh, sorry, Liz. Well, see you later. Bye."

Elizabeth shrugged. Apparently A.J. didn't know them well enough yet to tell them apart all the time, she reflected. Or maybe it was because Jessica was dressing so much like her lately. Jessica's hair was always back in a ponytail now, and by coincidence, both of them had worn jeans and pastel T-shirts that day.

Elizabeth turned to head for the *Oracle* office, but stopped and stood frowning in the middle of the hallway. It had finally sunk in that Jessica had actually asked A.J. to go to a Save the Whales meeting. For Jessica to be concerned about environmental issues—any issues—was like a heavy metal band playing lullabies. They just didn't go together.

She craned her neck and looked back in the direction in which A.J. had disappeared. "What is Jessica *doing*?" she muttered, shaking her head in bewilderment.

Deep in thought, Elizabeth headed for the newspaper office again. Jessica was acting very peculiar lately, and A.J. was a major part of the formula. Elizabeth had no idea what was going on.

Three

The distant shouts and laughter from kids playing outside drifted in through the open kitchen window as Elizabeth rinsed off spinach leaves for a salad. Her twin was chattering on the kitchen telephone with Lila about some "hideous" social error someone had made at school. That was typical of Jessica, Elizabeth thought. What wasn't typical was the way she had been acting around A.J. She was a completely different person whenever she was with him. Elizabeth decided her twin was acting like Dr. Jekyll and Mr. Hyde. It was almost spooky.

And what was even harder to understand was why Jessica thought her new personality was going to win A.J. over. Granted, A.J. had said he didn't like flirtatious girls, but that was no reason for Jessica to undergo an entire personality change. Elizabeth wanted to say something about it, but she had already tried once, and Jessica had been deeply offended. Her instincts told her it would definitely be a touchy subject to bring up again with her volatile twin.

After a screech of laughter, Jessica said goodbye to her friend and hung up the phone.

"Ugh, I can't believe it," she said, hopping down from her perch on the table. "It's really sickening the way they act," she concluded as she strolled over to join Elizabeth at the sink. "So, what's for dinner?"

Elizabeth shook the colander full of spinach and dumped it into a bowl. "Spinach salad and cold chicken," she replied. She started crumbling bacon into bite-size pieces and added, "Are you planning to set the table or what?"

"Of course I am. Calm down, Liz. I was just about to start," Jessica declared. Because their mother worked such long hours as an interior designer, the girls shared many of the household chores and took turns getting dinner ready and doing the dishes.

As she reached up into a cupboard for a stack of plates, Jessica commented, "You know, some of those people in the Save the Whales group take themselves so seriously—like Monica Bishop, for instance. Man, she thinks she's going to save the whole world, not just the whales."

Elizabeth frowned slightly while she sliced some mushrooms. That was just the opening she had been hoping for. "Well, that's because the people who belong to those environmental groups believe in them, Jess. Why, uh—did you go?"

"Because it's the kind of thing A.J. thinks I'm interested in, that's why. Let's eat outside tonight." Plates in hand, Jessica headed toward the patio door, which was off the dining room. As she came back inside, Prince Albert, the twin's golden Labrador retriever, followed her in. Jessica walked into the kitchen, clattered together forks and knives and grabbed a handful of paper napkins.

Elizabeth watched her silently for a moment. Then she let out a puzzled sigh. "Jess? I don't get it. Why does he think that, and why don't you just tell him it's not true?"

"Because, Liz." Dropping her eyes, Jessica leaned against the counter and shook her head. She suddenly looked worried. "Because A.J. is a pretty serious guy. He likes poetry and all that stuff. And he thinks I'm the sweet, thoughtful, sensitive type—you know, artistic, concerned about the environment."

"Well, you *are* sweet," Elizabeth pointed out in a gently cajoling tone. She popped a mushroom into her mouth and grinned. "But this whole shy and quiet routine you're doing—that's not the real you, Jess. Come on."

"A.J. wouldn't like the real me—I mean the *old* me," Jessica corrected herself as she turned away.

"What?" Perplexed, Elizabeth crossed the kitchen in three strides and took Jessica's arm. She jiggled her sister's elbow lightly. "Jessica! A.J. would be crazy not to like the real you, are you kidding? Why don't you give him a chance to find out what you're really like?"

But Jessica shook her head vehemently, sending her ponytail swishing back and forth. "I already told you. No way!"

Elizabeth was exasperated but also sympathetic to her sister's feelings. "Jess, why are you so sure he would only like you if you were soft and sweet and serious?"

Jessica raised her eyes to meet Elizabeth's for a moment, then turned away and began pleating a napkin into tiny folds. "I just know it, that's why. You remember how turned off he was when you were flirting with him to make Jeffrey jealous."

"That's true," Elizabeth agreed. "But, Jess, there are so many other great things about you. I know he'd like the real you if you gave him a chance."

Jessica shook her head emphatically. "Forget it, Liz! It's not a chance I feel like taking. And besides, I really have changed. I'm not like that anymore."

There was nothing Elizabeth could say in response to that. It was blatantly untrue; Jessica would always be Jessica, no matter what act she put on. Only two minutes earlier she had been gossiping with Lila just as always. Elizabeth stared at her sister's back, at a loss for words.

"Liz!" Instantly Jessica whirled around again, her blue-green eyes wide with panic. "You aren't going to do anything crazy like *tell* A.J. what I used to be like, are you?"

Elizabeth blinked in surprise. "Uh . . . no."

"Well, don't."

"I won't!"

"Promise? *Promise* you won't say anything at all to A.J., OK?"

The urgency in Jessica's voice went straight to Elizabeth's heart. She had never seen her twin so serious about a boy that she was willing to turn her whole life inside out. But the fact that Jessica *was* turning her life inside out worried her. It worried her a lot.

"Liz?"

Against her better judgment Elizabeth shrugged and nodded. "OK, Jess. If it's really that important to you, I won't say anything. I promise."

They stared at each other for a long moment. Already Elizabeth regretted her promise. Since she loved her sister so much—in spite of, or maybe because of her wild unpredictability and her outrageousness—she knew someone like A.J. would, too. But only if he had a chance. In reality, he had never even met Jessica Wakefield. And Elizabeth was aching to set things straight. Unfortunately, now her hands were tied.

Outside, a car door slammed, and then another, and Prince Albert let out a sharp, cheerful bark. He looked up from his bowl of dog food and turned expectantly toward the door with his tail wagging.

"Mom and Dad are home," Jessica said in a subdued voice. She sent Elizabeth another pointed glance and repeated, "Remember. You promised."

Repressing a sigh, Elizabeth nodded and went back to finish the salad. "I know. I won't say anything."

"So, how are my girls?" Ned Wakefield strolled into the Spanish-tiled kitchen and set his briefcase on the counter. "Something sure smells good."

Jessica greeted her father, then headed out to the picnic table again.

"Hi, Dad," Elizabeth said with a smile. She picked up a piece of bacon and handed it to him. "That's what you smell—for the spinach salad."

"Mmm. Is this cleared with your mom? She's trying to lower my cholesterol, you know." Dark-haired and handsome, Mr. Wakefield gave Elizabeth a twinkling grin and munched happily on the bacon. Prince Albert watched every mouthful disappear with pitiful longing in his brown eyes.

"It's approved in limited quantities," Elizabeth answered. "Where is Mom, anyway?"

"Here I am." Alice Wakefield backed into the kitchen with an armload of wallpaper books. She saw her husband furtively licking his fingers and gave him a mock scowl. "I saw that, Ned," she scolded as she set the books down on a chair and looked over at the plate of bacon. Inhaling deeply, she smiled at Elizabeth. "He doesn't get any more, sweetheart. Remember that."

"Yes, ma'am!" Elizabeth said, and then swatted at her father's hand as he reached for another slice. He chuckled silently and surrendered.

As her parents talked over what each of them had done at work, Elizabeth thought of how perfect they were together. Each of them did what was fulfilling and important to them. They treated each other as equals and never put on any kind of pretense.

Unlike Jessica and the way she's acting with A.J., she thought. Troubled, Elizabeth crumbled up the rest of the bacon and added it to the salad. If only Jessica would admit who she was and what she was like, Elizabeth was certain her twin could have a great relationship with A.J. Otherwise, it would never work.

After dinner Elizabeth went up to her room to practice her recorder. She had taken it up recently—after Jessica had started playing it to impress a music student and then abandoned it—and now she was really hooked. She had even invested in a better recorder than the one she originally borrowed from Jessica. Her friend Julie Porter, who was an advanced flute and piano player, had been coaching her. Now she used every chance she had to practice.

But as she repeatedly played a series of scales, her mind drifted back to Jessica's latest romantic intrigue. Her twin had done a lot of crazy things to get boys, but instinctively Elizabeth sensed that this one was much more serious than any of the others. And that meant Jessica was liable to get even more carried away than usual. At the moment, Elizabeth knew, her twin was in her room deeply absorbed in some mysterious, top-secret project. She suspected it was another plan for impressing A.J. Well, she wouldn't find out what it was unless Jessica decided to tell her. Shrugging, she focused on her music again and adjusted her fingers over the holes of the recorder.

"Liz? Can I talk to you for a second?" Jessica stuck her head through the bathroom door that connected their bedrooms. Her expression was tentative.

Elizabeth put her recorder down and smiled. "Sure, Jess. What's up?"

"Well . . ." Jessica walked into Elizabeth's bedroom. She held a sheet of paper in her hand. Taking a deep breath, she said, "I've been working on a poem, and I want to know what you think."

"A *poem*?" Elizabeth echoed in disbelief.

Her twin nodded eagerly. "Yeah, I'm going to start writing poetry every day from now on. A.J. loves poetry, remember?" With an enthusiastic grin, she held out a piece of paper. "I decided to do free verse 'cause I'm not very good at rhyming," she added modestly.

Something held Elizabeth back. On the one hand Jessica was really in love with A.J. But on the other hand she was taking things too far. Writing poetry wasn't Jessica's style, and it never would be. There was no sense pretending.

And knowing Jessica, Elizabeth doubted that

she was about to read a masterpiece. Actually, she didn't know what she was about to read, but she forced herself to keep an open mind for her sister's sake. Smiling reluctantly, she took the poem and read it.

Time is a grinding wheel of merciless pain
We are trapped in our lives
    until the hour of death.
But love breaks our chains and lets us fly
    into the universe
Where everything is real and alive
Forever.

Elizabeth kept her expression rigidly neutral as she read Jessica's poem. Nodding thoughtfully, she read it again and tried to come up with something encouraging to say about it. Unfortunately, all she could think to suggest was instant incineration.

"Well? What do you think? I want your absolutely, totally honest opinion, Liz. Don't say it's good just because I wrote it." Jessica looked at her with an optimistic smile. "So?"

"It's—umm . . . your images are—uh—they're good images," she faltered, putting as much enthusiasm into her voice as possible. She carefully avoided meeting her sister's eyes.

"What about the part about the universe?"

Jessica prodded. "You don't think that's too dramatic?"

"N-noo . . ."

"*Well*? What would you change? Go ahead, I don't mind. Be totally honest."

Elizabeth crossed to the table she used as a desk and sat down on the edge of the chair. She fiddled with a ballpoint pen for a few seconds to stall for time. "It starts out pretty—pretty sad," she began in a guarded tone. "But then it gets hopeful."

Jessica grinned exultantly. "I know. That's pretty good, huh? I worked on it for ages." Still smiling happily, Jessica bounced over to Elizabeth's side and gave her a quick hug. "Don't you think A.J. will be just blown away?"

Elizabeth's heart skipped a beat. "You're showing this to A.J.?" she echoed in a hollow voice.

Her sister nodded. "Uh-huh. I wrote it for him. It's really a love poem, you know. See, there's this stuff about love making us free."

"Right." Elizabeth swallowed hard and nodded.

"I wonder if I should make it longer," Jessica mused as she bent over the desk. "Think so?"

Inside, Elizabeth was in a turmoil. The critic in her thought the poem was terrible. But at the same time Jessica was so proud of herself for writing it, and so much in love with A.J. that she had labored over it for an hour. She just couldn't crush Jessica's excitement, but showing A.J. the poem could turn him off forever! Instead of sounding deep and intellectual, it sounded trite and depressing.

Beside her, Jessica let out a light, self-conscious laugh. "You know, it's really kind of amazing that I'm doing this. I mean, Jessica Wakefield writing love poems!"

"That's for sure."

"But I just know A.J.'s going to be impressed by how sensitive I am," Jessica went on dreamily. She propped her chin in her hands and gave Elizabeth a twinkling smile. "And, you know, I think I really am a pretty sensitive person, don't you?"

Elizabeth felt a surge of tenderness for her sister. She might be going about it the wrong way, but she certainly was sincere about winning A.J.'s admiration.

"Sure, Jess." Placing her hand on her twin's arm, she suggested tenderly, "Maybe I could help you write something a little bit lighter. You know, something sensitive, but with less emphasis on death and pain."

"You don't really like it, do you?"

"Sure I do," Elizabeth said hastily. "But maybe for the first poem you show him it could be more"—she cast around for the words that would con-

vince Jessica—"sweet and—and beautiful," she
urged.

A happy light came into Jessica's eyes. "Hey,
maybe you're right. Something sweet and beautiful. Oooh!" She hugged Elizabeth again im-
pulsively. "You're the greatest sister in the world,
Liz. How about something about a rainbow? Or
flowers?"

Smiling ruefully, Elizabeth pulled a notebook
toward her and reached for a pen. If she had to
write a love poem herself for Jessica, she would.
But privately she wished Jessica would drop the
whole idea and get back to being herself.

Four

"Where are my sneakers? Ohmigod! Liz?" In a breathless flurry Jessica stormed into Elizabeth's room through the bathroom, gripping a wet towel around her. She stared at her sister with wide, indignant eyes. "Have you seen my sneakers?"

Elizabeth, who was reading in bed in her nightgown, gave her a shrug. "Sorry. Haven't seen them."

"Ugh! A.J. will be here in approximately *seven* seconds, and I'm a total disaster!" Gritting her teeth, Jessica flounced back into the bathroom and flung open the medicine cabinet. She rattled through a huge assortment of makeup. Lip glosses and mascaras tumbled into the sink.

"Where is that eyeliner?" she muttered, clutching the towel still tighter around her body. Then she slammed the door shut. "Amy took it, I know it. I could *kill* her!"

As she yanked open a drawer by the sink and rummaged through the makeup that filled it to the top, her sister appeared in the bathroom doorway. "Why are you going to Secca Lake so early? The picnic doesn't start until twelve."

Jessica gave her a pained look. "A.J. and I are going hiking first, that's why. Have you seen that blue mascara I had?"

"Hiking? You're going hiking?"

"Yeah. What's wrong with that?" she asked indignantly. She met her twin's eyes and then looked away.

She had to admit, hiking wasn't exactly her favorite way to spend a Saturday morning. In fact, she preferred to stay in bed until peak tanning hours, as a rule, and then flop into a lounge chair by the pool. Minimum effort was usually her policy on the weekend. But hiking was the kind of healthy, outdoorsy thing that Elizabeth did, and Jessica was taking all her cues from her sister. That was what A.J. liked and expected. In fact, he had suggested the hike himself, so she had immediately agreed, even though the idea of trudging around Secca Lake didn't fill her with jubilation.

Elizabeth shrugged. "You've never really been interested in hiking before, that's all."

"Well, I am now."

Jessica hurried into her room and tossed the damp towel onto her bed. After quickly putting on her underwear and shorts, she ransacked her dresser for a short-sleeved, button-down khaki shirt her aunt had given her for Christmas. It wasn't really her style, but it fit the nice-girl image she was trying to project. She found it at the back of a drawer and hastily put it on.

"Hey, Liz? Have you seen the bird-watching guide?"

Following her into the room, Elizabeth gave Jessica an incredulous stare. "Bird-watching? *Jessica!* What is with you, anyway?"

Jessica eyed her sister narrowly. "*You* know," she muttered, dragging a brush through her hair. "And remember, you promised."

For a moment Elizabeth didn't say anything. But then she sighed. "Yeah, right, Jess."

Outside, a car honked. Letting out a shriek, Jessica raced to her closet and made one more frantic search for her sneakers. Miraculously this time she found them underneath her dirty cheerleading uniform.

She sent an agonized glance toward the window as she struggled to put them on. "Tell A.J. I'll be right there."

Elizabeth laughed and opened the window. "Since when did you care if you kept a guy waiting?" Leaning out, she called, "Hi, A.J.! She'll be down in a second!"

Jessica lunged to her feet, grabbed the family binoculars, which she had put on her bed, and raced out of her room. She pounded down the stairs and ran for the front door, then skidded to a halt. Taking a deep breath, she composed herself, smiled, and walked calmly outside.

Her heart fluttered excitedly when she saw A.J., who was leaning against the car, waiting for her. He grinned and raised one hand in a casual greeting, and Jessica smiled blissfully in response.

"Hi," she said, meeting his eyes. "Ready to go?"

"Yup. What are the binoculars for?" A.J. asked as they both climbed into his car.

"Bird-watching. I just love birds, don't you? I'm hoping we'll get a chance to see the—the, uh—" Jessica cut herself off as she realized she wasn't sure what kind of birds they might see at Secca Lake. But she wanted him to believe she was a dedicated nature lover, and bird-watching seemed like the perfect touch. She gave him a lightning smile. "The green-crested pod-eater," she fibbed.

A.J. gaped at her, a surprised expression on his face. "Green-crested pod-eater?"

"Yeah. It's very rare, but we might be lucky enough to see one."

He glanced at her again and then chuckled softly. "OK. We'll be on the lookout for the green-crested pod-eater."

Sighing contentedly, Jessica sat back and enjoyed the rest of the ride up to Secca Lake. *So far so good*, she told herself gratefully. *Just keep it up.*

When they arrived at the big state park, Jessica hopped out of the car and headed directly for the path that wound into the dense pine woods surrounding the lake. "Come on, there's a great view from Lookout Rock," she explained, grabbing A.J.'s hand and pulling him after her.

"How far is it?" he asked. He fell into step beside her, loping along with easy strides.

"Oh, maybe a mile," Jessica guessed. She gave him a ready-for-anything smile. "But we could go all the way around the lake if you want."

He let out a startled gasp, and his eyes took in the size of the lake, which stretched out in front of them. "You really want to? It's kind of far."

Jessica cursed herself silently. *What a stupid thing to say.* "Well . . ."

"And everybody else will probably be here way before we get back," he added, then shrugged apologetically. "Maybe some other time we could do the whole thing."

"Sure. Whatever." To herself, Jessica breathed a sigh of relief. But to A.J. she gave another bright, enthusiastic smile. She had definitely gotten off easy that time! "Well, let's go." She set off at a brisk pace, holding her binoculars. She was prepared to catch a glimpse of the pod-eater.

"I just love this place, don't you?" she said, puffing as she tramped along the path. "The lake is so beautiful, so inspiring. It really makes you aware of how incredible nature is, don't you think?"

A.J. nodded and swatted at a mosquito. "Yeah. It's really nice."

By reflex Jessica caught a branch just before it snapped back in her face, and she ground her teeth on a silent curse. She hoped they wouldn't have to go hiking too many times. She was already hot, sweaty, bug-bitten, and scratched, but there was no way she was going to let A.J. know what misery it was for her. As far as he was concerned, she was just loving her invigorating hike through the woods.

"This is great. This is just great," she lied, keeping her smile fixed on her face. "We should do this every weekend."

A.J. smiled back at her. "I'm glad you're having such a good time, Jess. Back in Atlanta I had a hard time finding hiking partners."

They trudged along in silence for a few minutes, until Jessica recognized the path that turned off to the shore. "Here, it's this way."

She led the way through the branches until they emerged at the edge of the lake. A house-size boulder jutted into the water, and they clambered up onto it. Once she was seated, Jessica put her binoculars up to her eyes. "I bet we could see, ah—those ducks. You know, those special ducks," she murmured, scanning the distant shore. "Isn't this beautiful?"

"See any green-crested pod-eaters?"

She shook her head. "Not yet, but I bet we— Wait a second! That could be— Oh, no! It's gone. Sorry." With a small apologetic smile, she handed A.J. the binoculars. "Too late."

"That's OK." Taking the binoculars, A.J. surveyed the lake and then turned them on Jessica. "Whoa! There's something."

Jessica blushed and turned away. For some reason A.J. always made her feel as if she were on her first date. She guessed that was what being in love was like. *You've got to make this work*, she told herself urgently. *It's got to work.*

"Want to keep going?" she piped up brightly.

A.J. shook his head. "How about we just hang out here for a while, just sit and talk. You know."

"Oh. Sure. We can just talk." As Jessica spoke, her mind raced ahead, choosing topics of conversation she thought A.J. would be interested in, topics that would show him what a serious, thoughtful person she was.

"You know," she began, "I was reading in the paper the other day about the world hunger situation. And it's really bad. I mean, all those people with nothing to eat except—" She hesitated. What was it that they ate?

"Rice?" A.J. supplied.

She nodded. "Right. Rice. I think we should all go for a whole week eating nothing but a bowl of cold rice once a day and see what it's like. Don't you think that's a good idea?"

"Well . . ." A.J. tipped his head to one side and twirled a pine needle between his fingers. "The truth is, lots of people don't even get that much. I don't know how the Peace Corps people can do it—eating every day when they're working with famine victims."

Jessica frowned, trying to come up with a

good response. Obviously A.J. had done some serious thinking about the subject. She wished she were better prepared to discuss it with him. "I was thinking about joining the Peace Corps myself. I'm definitely for peace," she added fervently.

A.J. gave her an odd look. "Actually, it's really hard work. I don't think I could hack it myself. It takes a lot of guts. You'd have to learn to do without a lot of the luxuries we take for granted."

"But we should try it, so we know what those people go through," she insisted, leaning forward with an earnest expression on her face.

A.J. nodded.

What did I do wrong? she was asking herself desperately. *He thinks I'm so stupid.*

Instinctively Jessica sensed that she wasn't grabbing his attention the way she wanted to. Maybe she just wasn't being interesting enough.

"It's just not fair, you know?" she went on, her voice quivering with intensity. "There's so much injustice in the world, and—and—"

"I know what you mean." A.J. smiled at her briefly but let out a tiny sigh.

Jessica swallowed hard and looked out across the water. For a moment she was tempted to recite her poem for him. That might do the trick. But something held her back. Some other time, maybe.

To her surprise A.J. reached for her hand. "You're a really special person, you know that?" he said in a soft voice.

A dizzy wave of bashfulness swept over Jessica, and she turned her face away. "Oh . . ." She was so confused she pulled her hand out of his grasp without thinking.

"Are you getting hungry?" A.J. asked in a slightly disappointed tone. He nodded back toward the way they had come. "I bet people are starting to show up by now."

"Sure, you're right," she replied. She felt a pang of regret. Their hike hadn't gone as well as she hoped it would, and she had just blown her first chance to get romantic. *How could I be so stupid?* she rebuked herself angrily.

But she managed a cheerful smile. "OK. Let's go. I'm starved."

"Didn't anybody bring paper towels or napkins? I got hamburger grease all over my hands!" Winston Egbert, a floppy chef's hat perched on his head, faced the crowd and gave a disgusted grimace. He shook the hamburger flipper for

50

emphasis. "Every time we do this there's something missing! You guys must have your brains in a permanent airlock. It's no ketchup or no cups or no—" He was shouted down boisterously.

Elizabeth turned to Jeffrey and gave him a teasing grin. "Hey, wasn't that supposed to be your department?" she whispered. "Paper napkins?"

Shaking his head, Jeffrey put one finger to his lips. "Say anything and you die," he growled softly, his green eyes dancing.

"I'll just wait until I want to blackmail you for something."

Cara Walker reached across the picnic table for the big bottle of soda next to Elizabeth. "Liz? Isn't Jessica coming today?" the pretty brunette asked. Cara was one of Jessica's good friends, and she also dated the twins' older brother, Steven, who was a freshman at a nearby state university. She had invited him to come to the picnic, but he had had to work on a paper.

"Mmm. She's already here somewhere," Elizabeth answered, munching on a potato chip. She glanced out at the lake and shrugged. "She and A.J. came early to do some hiking."

Cara gave her a pained look. "Hiking?"

"That's what I said to her," Elizabeth admitted.

"Well, this has got to be a first. There she is."

51

Turning quickly, Elizabeth saw her sister and A.J. emerge from the woods, looking tired, hot, and uncomfortable. At least that was the impression Elizabeth got from seeing her sister's face. Frowning, she watched Jessica and A.J. approach.

"Hey, you guys!" Roger Patman stood up on a bench and waved his hands for quiet. "Football game starts in two seconds. Shirts against skins. Come on—let's go."

"Count me out," Lila drawled, rolling her eyes.

"Me, too," Maria Santelli said, giggling. "I wouldn't want to get stuck on the wrong team, if you know what I mean."

All of the boys clambered off the picnic benches and headed for the big field, while the girls stayed put. DeeDee Gordon switched on a radio.

"Hey, nature girl," Amy called to Jessica. She grinned maliciously. "You look very elegant today."

Jessica flopped down onto the bench next to Elizabeth and let out a sigh of exhaustion. "Hi, yourself," she grumbled. She wore a world-weary expression as she poured herself a cup of soda and gulped it down. Sighing again, she stared out toward where the boys were playing football.

Elizabeth followed her sister's gaze to A.J. and remembered the odd expression each of them had worn as they joined the group.

"Everything OK?" she asked in an undertone.

Her sister shrugged. "Yeah. I guess so."

"How was hiking?"

"Horrible."

Suppressing a sigh of frustration, Elizabeth said, "Then why do it, Jess? This is just dumb."

"I *told* you, Liz," Jessica retorted, her voice tight with strain. She glanced over at A.J. again, and a quiver of emotion passed across her face. "I already told you."

Elizabeth opened her mouth to speak, but then shook her head without saying anything. No matter what, it seemed as though Jessica was determined to play a role in front of A.J., a role that she just wasn't meant for. And if Elizabeth was right in thinking that A.J. looked a little— she hated to admit it—bored, then Jessica was being her own worst enemy.

Elizabeth was dying to make everything perfect for her sister. All it would take was making sure A.J. knew what Jessica was really like. That way Jessica could drop the act and just be herself.

But I can't. I promised.

Sunk in gloom, Elizabeth stared out over the

water while the other girls' conversation rattled on around her. The part of her that was always sensitive to her identical twin's feelings knew that Jessica was feeling a little depressed.

When the burgers were cooked, the boys all trooped back, and Jessica immediately perked up.

"Who won?" she asked, beaming up at A.J. All around the table, people were sitting down and reaching for food. The noise level instantly rose ten decibels.

He was panting as he pulled his T-shirt on over his head. "We did."

"Great! Good going." Jessica's voice was chirpy and bubbly, and she smiled like the happiest person in the world.

"Hey, you guys! You know the fund-raiser show's coming up," Winston announced through a mouthful of hamburger, "to raise money to start a dance program. They're auditioning all kinds of dance and musical acts. No stand-up comics, though," he added, trying to look depressed. "We're being discriminated against." Everyone laughed.

Jessica sat up a little straighter, Elizabeth noticed, at the mention of the variety show. Her twin was a glutton for the limelight and pictured herself as a great actress. Just recently Jessica had had a major role in *You Can't Take It*

With You at school, and she had reveled in every minute of the attention—and applause.

There was an excited buzz of voices as everyone began talking about people who might audition. Elizabeth fully expected her sister to step in to take control and put herself in a starring role. But after a moment Jessica turned away and began a low conversation with A.J.

"Jessica? Are you going to try out for the show?" Sandra Bacon asked.

Surprisingly Jessica shook her head and let out a modest laugh. "No, I don't really like showing off like that," she replied, darting a glance at A.J. "Maybe I'll help out backstage, though. If they need me," she added.

"Speaking of shows," Lila put in, leaning toward Jessica. "You'll never guess what's happening at Lisette's."

Jessica arched her eyebrows into a polite, questioning expression. "What?"

"Well . . ." Grinning, Lila crossed her arms and lowered her voice conspiratorially. "You know that designer Nadine? She does all those great clothes Lisette's sells."

Lisette's was one of the most popular stores in the mall, and one of Jessica's absolute favorites. The store specialized in very stylish, trendy outfits that were astronomically expensive. Whenever she saved enough money, Lisette's was the first place Jessica ran to, to spend it. Of course, lately, she hadn't been wearing many of her Lisette's clothes. Mostly she had been borrowing Elizabeth's more conservative blouses and skirts.

There was an expectant pause. Then Jessica cleared her throat and shot A.J. another quick glance. "Yeah? What about it?"

"Lila, what?" Amy prodded impatiently.

"Well, Nadine is doing this promotion thing," Lila explained in her typical bored-to-death tone. "She's going to custom-design a wardrobe for the girl who fits her image the best—and there's going to be a fashion show to pick the winner."

Instantly Elizabeth looked at her twin to see how Jessica would take the news. A wardrobe custom-designed by Nadine qualified as one of those things Jessica would gladly kill for, as Elizabeth knew perfectly well. But to her surprise Jessica just shrugged her shoulders with a casual air.

"Oh, that's interesting, Lilà."

Lila snorted skeptically. "Interesting, Jess? Aren't you the tiniest bit dying to enter?"

"I don't know. That's not—really my style," Jessica said hesitantly. She raised pleading eyes to Elizabeth.

Elizabeth knew exactly what was going on in her sister's head: Jessica was dying to enter the

56

fashion show and get a crack at the free wardrobe, but the Nadine image clashed with the one Jessica had been projecting lately. Obviously she didn't know how to get the stylish, flashy clothes and still convince A.J. she was a sweet, demure, and serious girl.

"Who knows?" Elizabeth put in brightly. "It could be fun to see what it's like, don't you think, Jess? Just as a joke." She was trying to let Jessica act as though it would just be a whim to enter, instead of deadly serious competition.

Giving her a grateful smile, Jessica looked away and shrugged. "I guess it could be—just for kicks. We'll see."

Five

A.J. jogged along in ankle-deep water while Jessica kept up a stream of conversation at his side. Every once in a while he nodded, or added a comment when necessary, but mostly his thoughts wandered.

Since he had started seeing Jessica, they had spent nearly every afternoon and weekend going to museums, attending meetings, having discussions, or going jogging on the beach. Not that he minded any of those things—he had even suggested the hiking and jogging. But it seemed that the instant he mentioned something he liked, Jessica immediately wanted to do it. It was beginning to make him hesitate to bring up anything new. He didn't know how many more activities they could possibly have time for.

As it was, they were constantly doing *something* now, instead of sometimes just goofing around or hanging out with friends. It was only Wednesday, but they had already packed the week full of activity. He was beginning to wonder if Jessica would ever stop taking everything so seriously and just relax for a minute.

"The ocean is incredible, isn't it?" Jessica said, gasping for breath and sweeping one arm out toward the far blue horizon. "It makes you realize how huge the universe is, doesn't it?" She turned her face toward his as they jogged along in the shallows, and a smile lit her luminous, blue-green eyes.

"Yeah, you've got a point there. The Pacific really makes you think, doesn't it?"

Her eyes shone. "Exactly! I just love running on the beach. I feel so in tune with life."

Smiling absently, A.J. nodded and concentrated on breathing steadily as the saltwater splattered his bare legs.

It was so strange, he thought to himself, that Jessica had turned out to be so different than he expected. She was so serious and responsible that sometimes he felt that he couldn't really act like himself when she was around. He didn't think he could flirt with her or tease her at all, in case she was offended. A lot of the time she made him feel he should be raising money for cancer research or attending lectures on nuclear disarmament—and that feeling was hard to handle.

And it wasn't that he didn't like girls who had more on their minds than clothes and gossip and partying. He really admired Jessica for being concerned about important issues. But she was so solemn and conscientious all the time that she was actually a bit boring. It was hard to believe, when he looked at the beautiful, graceful girl jogging along beside him. But that was the truth. All she seemed to want to do was talk about depressing problems, or do homework or some other virtuous thing. He was beginning to have second thoughts about going out with her.

It's too bad, though. I really thought we were going to hit it off.

"And then I couldn't decide if I should volunteer at the day-care center or help raise money for the new library," Jessica was saying. "I don't know, it just seems like—"

"What was that?" A.J. splashed to a halt and grabbed Jessica's arm. A faint noise had reached his ears.

"What? I didn't—"

"Shhh!" A.J. turned to scan the water. The ocean was a bit choppy, and it was hard to see anything clearly with the sun slanting into his eyes. He squinted against the glare and then tilted his head to catch the slightest sound. Then he heard it again and finally made out a dark figure bobbing in the waves and gesturing helplessly.

"What is it?"

"There! There's someone out there," he said, stripping off his T-shirt. He turned to Jessica and shoved his towel and shirt into her arms. "I've got to try and rescue whoever it is."

Jessica's eyes were wide with alarm. "OK," she whispered.

Without another thought A.J. ran straight into an oncoming wave and set out with strong strokes for the helpless person floundering in the surf.

On the shore Jessica stood rooted to the sand, with both hands pressed against her cheeks. Water washed up around her ankles as she watched A.J. reach the struggling person. Both heads disappeared beneath the waves for a heart-stopping moment, then bobbed up again. A.J., one arm supporting the tired swimmer, began swimming back toward shore.

Soon Jessica was able to make out the person A.J. had saved. It was a girl, about her own age, with dark curly hair. She was clinging tightly to A.J., and Jessica could see him speak to her reassuringly. In moments they were wading through the shallow waves. Bursting with curiosity, Jessica splashed down to meet them.

"What happened? Are you OK? Are you all right, A.J.?"

He nodded tersely and put one arm around the girl to support her as she lost her balance in a pounding wave.

"I-I'm fine," the girl sputtered, leaning heavily on A.J. She nodded and looked up into his face.

Now that Jessica could get a close look, she saw with a sting of irritation that the girl was extremely beautiful, with a voluptuous body scantily clad in a red bikini. Her dark hair streamed across her shoulders, and her thickly lashed huge blue eyes were turned to A.J. with gratitude.

"Everything OK?" Jessica repeated in a slightly less concerned tone.

"Yes, I'm—I'm fine." The girl caught her breath at last but continued to cling tightly to A.J.'s arm. "I had a cramp, and I didn't know the current was so strong, and I—"

"Hey, it's OK," A.J. broke in gently. He gave her a warm smile. "Don't worry. You're safe now."

She returned his smile and nodded solemnly. "You saved my life."

A fiery blush swept across A.J.'s cheeks. "Oh—I—"

"No, you did, you really did!" The girl glanced once at Jessica and gave her a quick, challenging look before turning her body back toward A.J. "I can never thank you enough," she murmured.

Jessica felt a jolt of indignation when she recognized the calculating gleam in the girl's wide blue eyes. Everything about her—her body language, the way she was looking at A.J.—told Jessica the girl was about to go after A.J. like a big-game hunter. Obviously she was the type of girl who liked to go after other girls' boyfriends. Jessica could see it in an instant.

But in order to keep in character with the role she had been playing, she couldn't do anything but be sweet and sympathetic. "Gee," she said, swallowing her anger, "it's so lucky we were here."

The girl ignored her but kept looking up at A.J. "It sure was."

A.J. was still blushing with embarrassment and pleasure. "What's your name?"

"Pamela Janson. I go to Whitehead Academy," the girl said with a smile.

Whitehead Academy was the exclusive private girls' school just up the coast in Bridgewater. Jessica could guess what Pamela was like:

64

spoiled, rich, used to getting what she wanted. And there was no doubt in Jessica's mind that Pamela wanted A.J.

"Well, maybe you shouldn't swim around here anymore," Jessica couldn't resist saying. She smiled demurely at Pamela, but she could tell her message got through.

Unfortunately, it didn't have any effect. Instead, Pamela moved a bit closer to A.J. and raised one limp hand to her heart. "I'm still so—I feel so weak. Could you just help me to my car?"

"Sure! No problem. Jessica? Let me have my towel. Pamela's shivering."

"Sure, A.J.," Jessica replied smoothly, giving him a concerned smile. As he turned his back to wrap it around Pamela, Jessica met the other girl's eyes. They exchanged a look that would have shocked him if he saw it. But he didn't.

"I'm parked over there," Pamela said, linking one arm through A.J.'s and deliberately leading him away from Jessica.

Her teeth on edge, Jessica trudged behind them. She watched in speechless fury as Pamela brushed up against A.J., hung on his arm, and sent him heartfelt smiles of gratitude with her pouting, sensuous lips. Under any other circumstances Jessica would have told Pamela to get lost. But as it was, she couldn't say or do anything at all that would look to A.J. as if she wasn't just as genuinely concerned and happy he had rescued Pamela as he was.

"This is it," Pamela crooned. She let her hand slip down into A.J.'s and nodded toward a white Mercedes convertible pulled up against the parking lot rail.

"Wow! Great car!"

Pamela threw her head back and let out a tinkling laugh. "Oh, I guess so. I really don't care what I drive, to tell you the truth. Cars are all the same to me." She looked up at A.J. through her thick, dark lashes, somehow making the simple statement heavy with romantic significance.

"Yeah, nice car, Pamela," Jessica echoed dryly. Inside, she was burning with envy. She had to exercise restraint to keep herself from forcibly prying Pamela's fingers off A.J.'s arm. Pamela wasn't just flirting, she was hooking into A.J. like a vampire.

"A.J.—A.J. what? What's your last name?" Pamela looked up at him with a blinding smile. She let her hand fall innocently on his, as he held the door for her.

"Morgan. A. J. Morgan."

"Thank you so much, A. J. Morgan," she repeated in a purring, seductive voice.

"I'm just glad we were there when you needed

us, that's all." He darted a look at Jessica and carefully slipped his hand out from under Pamela's.

Jessica nodded quickly. "Yeah, me, too. What a close call."

Still smiling, she watched Pamela sink gracefully into the driver's seat and toss her damp hair back across her shoulders.

"Bye. And thanks again, so much," Pamela said, starting up the convertible. "You're so strong and brave. Next time I hope there's someone just like you waiting to come to my rescue!"

A.J.'s eyes sparkled at her flattery. "No problem. But there won't be a next time, Pamela. At least I hope not—I mean—I hope you won't need *rescuing* again," he corrected himself.

"Me, too," Jessica put in. She met Pamela's arch look with a wide smile that didn't reach her eyes.

Gunning the powerful engine, Pamela gave A.J. one last, lingering look. When he turned away in confusion, she narrowed her blue eyes at Jessica and gave her a sly grin. Then she backed up and pulled away. Silent, they stood staring after her. A.J. looked as if he were in a daze.

Even though she was still smiling, Jessica's heart was flip-flopping painfully over the look on A.J.'s face. Swallowing hard, she repeated in the same bright tone, "Sure is lucky we were here."

Finally A.J. seemed to snap out of the trance he was in, and he looked at Jessica with an earnest nod. "You're not kidding. She could've drowned, you know. What if we'd been running up the beach the other way?" He shook his head in amazement.

Privately, Jessica wished they had been at least a hundred miles inland, looking east. But she couldn't let A.J. see what was really in her heart, so she shook her head in sympathy and said nothing.

A.J. let his breath out slowly and gave Jessica a questioning look. "I guess we might as well go, huh?"

"Sure. It's getting late," she agreed automatically. Deep in thought, she fell into step at his side, darting him quick, anxious looks.

"Pamela sure is—self-confident," she ventured. *Pushy* and *aggressive* was more like it, she said to herself. But the Jessica A.J. knew wouldn't say anything so unkind.

"Yeah—I mean, she does come on pretty strong," A.J. stammered.

"I guess. She's awfully pretty, too," Jessica added.

"In an obvious kind of way, though." They

reached A.J.'s car and climbed in, both absorbed in their thoughts.

Frowning in confusion, Jessica slammed her door and leaned against it, sending him another brief, worried look. If he really meant it—that he thought Pamela came on too strong—then that just underlined the fact that Jessica had to continue to act the way she had been in order for him to like her. But if that was true, why had he glowed with such pleasure when Pamela spoke to him?

A.J. started up the car and gave Jessica a soft smile. "I guess it's a good thing we came jogging today, huh?"

Meeting his eyes, Jessica nodded and forced a smile in return. "Yeah. Great."

Six

The telephone started ringing just as A.J. opened the front door of his house on Thursday afternoon. After tossing his books on the hall table, he ran into the kitchen and grabbed the phone.

"Hello?"

"Is this A.J.? A. J. Morgan?" a familiar voice asked.

A jolt of adrenaline raced through A.J. "Yes." He waited to be told what he already knew.

"Hi, this is Pamela Janson from the beach. Remember me?"

"Sure," he croaked. A dozen images flashed through A.J.'s mind at the sound of her voice. Somehow her tone promised excitement, even when she said the simplest things. He forced himself to sound casual. "What's up?"

"Well," she purred, "I was so upset yesterday, I didn't even realize I left with your towel, A.J. Wasn't that dumb of me? I've got it right here."

"Oh."

A.J. winced at himself for sounding so lame.

"And I was wondering . . . maybe you could come over? I'd bring it to your house, except I told my parents about how you saved my life, and they really want to meet you. I'm at home right now."

Every instinct told A.J. to say no. Earlier in the day he had made plans to meet Jessica at the library after her cheerleading practice, and he suspected that if he went over to Pamela's house first, somehow Jessica would end up hurt. He cleared his throat. "Well, that's OK, Pamela. I don't really need—"

"Don't you *dare* say no," she interrupted with a coy laugh. "They almost think I made the whole thing up, A.J., can you believe it? I need you to prove it really happened. Please?" she urged, her voice silky and hypnotic.

A picture of Jessica appeared in A.J.'s mind, bent over her books with a serious frown, and then a mental image of glamorous, sexy Pamela replaced it. Normally, girls who came on the way Pamela did turned him off. But lately he was beginning to wish his love life was a little more exciting.

Why shouldn't I? his conscience nagged. *It's not like I'm committed to Jessica or anything.*

"Well, uh . . ." He glanced over his shoulder nervously, as if he expected Jessica to be standing in the kitchen doorway. "It's just that I have to be somewhere later," he began.

"No problem. We're only fifteen miles up the coast. It'll just take a few minutes."

A.J. shrugged. There wasn't anything to get so worked up over, he reasoned. All he had to do was introduce himself, say a few polite words, and leave. Agonizing about Jessica was totally unnecessary.

"OK, sure. I'll just stop by, say hello, and go, how's that?"

There was a pause before he heard Pamela let out a quiet laugh. "OK, A.J. Great. Now, take the Coastal Highway . . ."

The Jansons' stark, dramatic house seemed to perch perilously on the rocks. A.J. pulled up next to Pamela's white Mercedes and let out a low whistle. Even from the driveway the view of the Pacific was breathtaking. Expertly landscaped terraces merged with the craggy slope going down to the beach, and the gray stone house almost seemed to grow up out of the rocky land. It looked as if it belonged there, but A.J.

knew it had probably cost a small fortune to create that impression.

Drawing a deep breath, he climbed out of the car and strolled up to the front door. A chime sounded distantly when he pressed the door bell. While he waited, he studied the patterns raked into the gravel of the small Japanese garden by the entrance and tried to look calm.

The door opened suddenly, catching him off guard. Pamela stood in front of him, dark, curly tendrils of hair framing her face. She was wearing a clingy white sun dress that showed every curve of her body, and a primitive necklace of wooden beads that emphasized the smoothness of her deeply tanned throat. For a moment she just looked at him, and then she gave him a big smile and reached for his arm.

"A.J.! Hi, come on in."

Forcing a smile, A.J. said, "Hi, Pamela. Nice —house."

She was leading him through a slate-floored foyer that was almost as big as the Morgans' living room. Her hips swayed seductively as she walked in front of him, and she cast a teasing look at him over one bare shoulder. "Daddy likes to show off," she drawled.

"Where are your folks?" A.J. asked.

Pamela didn't answer. She sauntered through an archway into the living room, where immense picture windows overlooked the ocean. Sinking gracefully onto a leather couch, she curled her legs up under her and shook her head.

"They're not home yet. You don't mind, do you?"

A.J. stood in the middle of the room, his heart pounding. For a moment all he could do was look around—anywhere but at Pamela. Modern paintings added bright splashes of color on the stone walls, and soft jazz was playing from hidden speakers. Everything was opulent, luxurious, and inviting. Especially Pamela.

He managed to swallow and gave her a nonchalant shrug. "No problem." So far, she didn't seem to be in a hurry to give him his towel.

"Why don't you sit down, A.J.?" Pamela gave him a smile, her blue eyes sparkling, and patted the sofa next to her.

"OK. Sure." He perched awkwardly on the edge of the couch a few feet away from her and glanced out the window. "This is really a fantastic house, Pamela. What a great place to live."

Pamela toyed with her necklace, twining it around her fingers as she stared at him.

"What time did you say your parents would be here?" he asked hoarsely, turning to meet her gaze.

She shrugged, "Actually, I don't know. They're out of town—in Denver, I think."

"What?" A.J. spoke in a whisper, and he could feel the heat in his cheeks. Obviously it was all a deliberate lie to get him there. And if there was one thing A.J. hated, it was that kind of game-playing. At least, he usually hated it. But at the moment he had to admit it was pretty flattering, too. Half of him wanted to leave, and the other half of him wanted to stay right where he was.

"Oh, uh—maybe I should—come back some other time," he stammered. He found himself staring at her as if he were hypnotized.

"But, A.J., you're already here," she murmured, scooting close to him. She trailed one finger along the back of his hand and then raised her eyes. "Stay." As she moved closer, one shoulder strap slipped off her tanned shoulder.

Mute, A.J. nodded. He felt as if he were in a dream and things were happening that were beyond his control. But he also felt that if he didn't put the brakes on fast, *everything* would be out of his control.

Abruptly he stood up and crossed to one of the big windows. He was blind to the view outside. "Do you think I could have something to drink?"

"Sure. A glass of wine, maybe?"

"Soda'd be fine," he said hastily. "Or juice or something."

She shrugged and sent him a lazy smile. "OK. I'll get you some soda."

As Pamela left the room, A.J. kept his eyes firmly fixed on a sailboat skimming offshore. *I should just leave*, he told himself frantically.

In the back of his mind, he still felt a certain amount of loyalty to Jessica. Even if he didn't think the relationship was going to work, he couldn't just shrug her off this way. He owed her more than that. And besides, if there was a remote possibility that things would get better, it was still worth a shot. So before *something* ended up happening between him and Pamela, he knew he should leave. But he couldn't move.

He heard the tinkling of ice when Pamela came back, and he pulled himself away from the window with effort. "Thanks," he said, taking the glass from her without meeting her eyes. He gulped thirstily as a way of putting off any more conversation.

"You get the same view from the greenhouse," she said huskily. She was standing so close, he could feel the warmth of her body. "That's where the hot tub is."

"Oh—really?"

"Mmm-hmm. . . . Want to relax in the tub while we wait for my parents?"

A.J.'s mind raced, and he looked rapidly around the room as though searching for an escape route. "Well, I don't have a bathing suit with me," he faltered.

With a soft, throaty chuckle, Pamela shook her head so her curls swished across her bare shoulders. "That doesn't matter."

"Oh, well . . ." Blushing fiercely, A.J. took another desperate swallow of his soda, then shook his head wistfully. "I—I don't think so. I probably should leave pretty soon anyway."

"I didn't think you were so shy, A.J.," Pamela murmured, looking at him through her lashes. "You weren't shy yesterday when you put your arms around me."

"That—that was different. I was pulling you to shore—"

"And you were so strong and brave, too."

Giving a short, self-conscious laugh, A.J. shook his head and backed up. Pamela's smile was too alluring, too daring. His resistance was wearing paper-thin. "Listen, I *really* have to go now."

She folded her arms across her chest and pouted. "You're leaving me all alone?" she said in a pleading little-girl voice. The look in her eyes was anything but little-girl.

"Yeah—I just have to go, that's all. I'm sorry."

After a moment Pamela shrugged and dropped back onto the couch. "OK," she said with a sigh. "But before you go, I want to ask you something. Whitehead is having a dance in a couple of weeks. Would you come?"

A.J. stood in the middle of the room, torn by conflicting emotions. There was no denying that Pamela was a beautiful, sexy girl who obviously seemed to like him. Everything she had done and said that afternoon proved that. But on the other hand, there was Jessica.

"Can I tell you in a few days?" he asked hesitantly.

"A few days?" she repeated softly. Her lips curved up in a knowing smile. "OK, A.J. You don't have to decide right this minute."

He let out a sigh of relief. "Good. Look, I've really got to go," he repeated, setting his empty glass down on a table. He gave her an uncertain smile. There was no telling what she might try next. "Can I have my towel?"

"Sure. It's in my room."

A.J. stayed where he was and looked steadily at the floor.

Finally Pamela sighed and pushed herself up. "I'll go get it."

In a few minutes she returned and tossed his

beach towel at him. He caught it and swung it over his shoulders. "Thanks. I'll see you around."

"Bye, A.J. Don't forget about that dance. I'm counting on you."

He smiled briefly and headed for the door. "I'll let you know, Pamela. Thanks for the soda."

As A.J. let himself out of the house, he had a feeling of having escaped by a very narrow margin. He didn't know how long he had been there, but it felt like years. Stooping into his car, he caught a glimpse of the dashboard clock and let out a groan. He was supposed to have met Jessica at the library twenty minutes earlier.

"Oh, no," he whispered, starting up the car. "What am I *doing*?"

He glanced at the house one more time. Pamela was leaning in the doorway, and her lazy half-smile seemed to say, "You'll be back."

A.J. swallowed hard and backed out of the driveway, then headed for Sweet Valley, where Jessica was waiting.

Seven

Fuming with aggravation, Jessica slumped down in her chair and drummed her pencil on the table. She darted a look at the door and then glanced at the wall clock again. Normally time was irrelevant to Jessica. She never cared if she was late getting somewhere, because as far as she was concerned, things didn't get started until she showed up anyway. But the one thing she hated more than anything else was to be kept waiting, especially when she had been on time. A.J. was already half an hour late.

"Where is he?" she muttered, crossing her arms on her chest. She scowled across the quiet library and clenched her jaw.

As long as she stayed angry, she wouldn't start worrying. But it wouldn't be long before a real anxiety attack set in, she knew. She didn't want to think about *why* A.J. was so late.

She cast a brief, surreptitious look around the library and then pulled the latest issue of *Ingenue* out of her bag. Quickly flipping through the pages, she noted all the Nadine fashions. Ever since Lila had told her about the fashion show and contest, she hadn't been able to get it out of her head. Lately there were only two topics on her mind: winning A.J. and winning a wardrobe of Nadine designs. But she wasn't sure she could do both.

Stifling a sigh, she sat upright and propped her chin up on her fists. Her eyes strayed to the door again, and a flicker of annoyance and embarrassment passed across her face as Amy and Lila strolled in. One thing she didn't need was Lila and Amy finding out that she was waiting for a boy. But they caught sight of her and headed for her table.

"Hi, Jess," Lila whispered.

Amy hopped into a seat next to her, her eyes alight with curiosity. "Hi. What are you doing?"

"Homework," Jessica replied succinctly. She certainly wasn't going to tell them she was being stood up.

"Us, too." Amy groaned. "We have to photocopy some stuff out of the encyclopedia—major headache."

Lila sat in a lounging position in an armchair, dangling one manicured hand over the back.

She looked around her with a faintly disgusted air. With a world-weary sigh, she turned to Jessica and drawled, "So, what's the story with this contest at Lisette's? You're going to be in it, right?"

Dropping her eyes to her notebook, Jessica fiddled with a pencil to stall for a moment. More than anything, she wanted to be in the contest. She was a natural to win it. But secretly she was afraid A.J. was slipping from her grasp. His lateness today seemed to prove that. She didn't want to do anything to jeopardize the relationship at this point, and she was afraid he might think she was vain and clothes-conscious if she signed up.

"Well, I—I don't know. Maybe," she said reluctantly. "I'm still thinking about it."

"You don't *know*? I can't believe you're saying this," Amy scoffed. She scooted her chair closer to Jessica and looked into her face. "Listen, Jess. You've just got to be in it. I know you could win."

"Why don't *you* enter?" Jessica asked.

Amy grimaced. "Because Nadine's clothes always make me look fat, for some bizarre reason, that's why."

"They don't make me look fat," Jessica grumbled, slumping down in her seat again.

"Come on, Amy. Let's get that stuff photocopied," Lila cut in impatiently. "I don't want to be stuck here all day, you know."

"OK, OK. Do it, Jess, huh? Just do it." After giving Jessica a firm look, Amy pushed herself out of her chair and followed Lila to the reference section.

Jessica tried not to look at the clock again. She was really starting to panic. What if A.J. didn't come at all? That would be the end.

A few minutes later Jessica saw Amy and Lila heading for the exit. As they pushed open the door, someone bumped into them on the way in. There was a muffled exclamation, and Amy shot a questioning look back at Jessica. Then they were gone, and A.J. was hurrying toward her.

Instantly Jessica forced a cheerful, unconcerned smile and sat up straight in her chair. She prayed it wasn't obvious that her heart was pounding painfully and that she felt like shouting at the top of her lungs, "Where have you been?"

"Jessica, I'm so sorry," he began before he even sat down. He was breathing hard, as though he had run from the parking lot. He slid his books onto the table, pulled out a chair, and sat down. "I'm really, really sorry I'm late."

"That's OK. I was just working on my math homework. I didn't even realize you were late," she lied, still smiling angelically.

"Yeah, but I am late," he repeated. He glanced off across the library for a moment and twitched his shoulders nervously.

Jessica felt a little bit mollified that he was so sorry and apologetic. Maybe things weren't so bad after all. "Hey, really," she insisted. "It's OK."

His eyes met hers, and he shook his head a fraction. "It's—see, I had to stop off at that girl's house—Pamela?"

Jessica's smile froze. While a dozen heartbeats pounded in her rib cage, she stared at A.J. with a stunned expression in her eyes. It was actually *worse* than her worst fears. Of all the reasons to be late, being with another girl was the most unacceptable. She had a nagging fear that disaster was about to strike. "Yeah?" she prompted, her mouth dry.

A.J. looked away from her. "She called me at home and said she had taken my towel yesterday by mistake, and she wanted me to come over and pick it up and meet her folks, so I did. That's all," he finished in a rush.

I bet she took it on purpose, Jessica seethed inwardly. At that moment Pamela Janson moved up to the top of her Most Hated list. But Jessica remained sympathetic and understanding on the outside.

"Oh, that's all," she said, forcing her mouth

into a smile. "I bet her parents were happy to meet you."

To her surprise A.J. looked very uncomfortable. "Well—they weren't actually—there," he faltered.

She let a few dull heartbeats go by again. "They weren't?"

"No. Pamela thought they'd be home by the time I got there, but they weren't."

Jessica thought she would explode if she had to hold in her anger and outrage much longer. It was perfectly obvious to her that Pamela was deliberately trying to steal A.J. away from her, and she was using the most outrageous tricks to do it, too. They were the same tricks that Jessica had often used before. But she swore Pamela was not going to succeed.

"Oh, that's too bad," she said. Her stomach muscles hurt from holding herself under control. Forcing herself to smile, she added, "Pamela was nice to call you, too. She could have just kept the towel."

A.J. fingered his jaw and kept his eyes on the table. He didn't want to look up at her, that was obvious.

For a moment Jessica thought she might burst into tears. Staying friendly and sweet meant she couldn't fight back the way she wanted to, and it just wasn't fair. She ached to point out to

A.J. that he was being manipulated and chased and that Pamela was probably just doing it to boost her own ego. Once she had snared A.J., she was likely to dump him in a week. Jessica knew the type only too well. But she couldn't say anything.

And she didn't think she could keep up her cheerful exterior anymore that afternoon. It was getting to be just about impossible not to scream or cry or do something equally drastic.

Glancing casually at the clock, she let out a disappointed exclamation. "Oh, no! I have to go now, A.J. I'm really sorry—"

"It's my fault for being late," he interrupted hastily. His brown eyes were troubled as he looked at her. "I'm the one who's sorry."

"Oh, forget it." Dismissing it all with a good-natured shrug, she scooped up her books and stood up. "I've got the Fiat, so I don't need a ride home. See you tomorrow in school, OK?"

A.J. nodded slowly, his forehead creased. "OK, Jessica. Bye."

Jessica kept her smile in place as she walked across the library and out the door. But by the time she had reached the convertible, hot, angry tears were spilling down her face faster than she could brush them away.

*　　*　　*

Elizabeth was practicing her recorder in her bedroom when the front door slammed downstairs. Absently she noted that her twin was home and turned to the next page in her lesson manual.

Without warning, her door flew open, and Jessica stood on the threshold, her face streaked with tears. "Oh, Liz!" she wailed.

"Jess! What's wrong?" Elizabeth jumped up and ran to her sister.

"A.J.—and he's—and Pam-Pamela is such a dirty sneak," Jessica choked. "And I have to—and it's not fair—but I w-w-*wanted* to—"

Elizabeth gently brushed Jessica's hair away from her face. "Jess, I can't understand a word you're saying! Can't you stop crying and tell me what happened?"

With effort Jessica drew a shaky breath and passed the back of one hand across her wet cheek. "You know this girl Pamela I told you about yesterday?"

Nodding, Elizabeth led her sister to the bed and sat her down. "Yeah. The man-eater. What did she do now?"

"She called A.J.—I know she took it on purpose—and asked him to go to her house—"

"Took what on purpose?"

Jessica's mouth tightened into a hard line. "His towel. I know she kept it deliberately so she'd have a good excuse to call him."

"Go on."

"So, anyway, he was supposed to meet me at the library, and he was over half an hour late," Jessica explained. Her chin quivered dangerously as she added, "And I know she was just working on him like crazy. And I know she's just doing it for kicks, Liz. She doesn't care about him the way I do!"

Elizabeth studied her twin in silence for a moment. Poor Jessica was sniffling miserably, her eyes still filled with tears. In spite of her promise to go along with Jessica's act, Elizabeth couldn't help saying, "You know, Pamela is no match for the real Jessica."

Her sister sent her a pained look.

"Come on, Jess. Let A.J. see what you're really all about," Elizabeth urged, taking Jessica's hand in hers. "He'd never even look at another girl if you did."

"I can't. It's too late now. This is the way he thinks I really am," Jessica said in a low voice. She shook her head emphatically. "I just can't change now. It would look too bizarre."

Deep in thought, Elizabeth sat, trying to figure out the best thing to do. Obviously, the best thing to do would be for Jessica to give up the charade. But that wasn't an option as far as Jessica was concerned.

Suddenly tears started running down Jessica's cheeks again, and her face crumpled. "What am I going to do, Liz? I like A.J. so much! I really want him to like me!"

"Oh, Jess." Elizabeth put her arms around her sister and hugged her tightly. "I told you what you should do, and you don't want to do it."

"I just can't," Jessica repeated stubbornly into Elizabeth's shoulder.

"Well, at least I know something that'll make you feel better. I can't guarantee it'll straighten things out with A.J., but it'll make you happy."

Jessica sat up, sniffling. "What?"

With a hopeful smile Elizabeth said, "Enter the fashion show, Jess! Come on, you really should." Her eyes sparkled with enthusiasm as she looked into her sister's face.

Frowning, Jessica balled up a damp tissue. "You really think it's a good idea?"

"Yes! Definitely! You look so great in those Nadine styles, Jess. I really mean it."

Jessica was clearly wavering. "You don't think A.J. will think I'm—the wrong type if I enter?"

Elizabeth shook her head vehemently. "No way. How could being in a fashion contest be something he wouldn't like? Come on, Jess! He isn't that conservative. And he'd think it was great if you won. Really," she repeated earnestly. "I bet he'd be proud of you."

"I really would love those clothes," Jessica began. She bit her lower lip for a moment. "And I guess . . ."

"Yes. You guess yes," Elizabeth cut in.

Jessica gave Elizabeth a thin, watery smile. "I guess I will. Maybe I'll even win, too."

Laughing, Elizabeth leaned forward to give Jessica another hug. "I know you will, Jess. Sign up on Saturday. Just do it."

"OK, I will," Jessica decided in a firmer voice. She sniffed hard and wiped away the last of her tears. "Thanks, Lizzie."

Elizabeth smiled and nodded. Privately, Elizabeth was hoping that being part of the contest would bring Jessica back to her old self. If it was exciting enough, and competitive enough, Jessica would use all her formidable powers to win. And that would be the *real* Jessica Elizabeth missed so much, the one Elizabeth wanted A.J. to meet before it was too late.

Eight

On Saturday morning Jessica, Lila, and Amy piled into the Fiat convertible and drove to the mall. It was a beautiful day, and with the crisp ocean breeze blowing through her hair, Jessica felt her spirits lifting. Signing up to win the custom-designed Nadine wardrobe couldn't do any harm, she reasoned happily. She decided she had just been acting paranoid when she worried whether A.J. would think less of her for doing it.

"This is the best thing you've done in about a million years," Amy said, echoing Jessica's thoughts. She pulled a strand of hair out of her mouth and grinned. "I know you'll win it, too."

"I hope so!" Jessica replied, laughing aloud.

Amy shifted on Lila's lap and nodded eagerly. "You're exactly the image they want, Jess.

The Modern Girl who knows what she wants—self-confident, strong, and independent. That's you, Jess."

"Usually," Lila corrected in an undertone. She shrugged as Jessica darted her a sour look.

"So listen. Now that you're doing this, think you'll try out for the fund-raising show, too?" Lila prompted. She had to shout over the rush of the wind. "You were great in *Splendor in the Grass* and *You Can't Take It with You*."

Jessica wrinkled her nose and signaled to turn into the Sweet Valley Mall parking lot. "I don't know." She had had a leading role in a couple of school plays, and she loved the applause and being in the spotlight. But things were different now. Before she did anything, she had to consider A.J. and what he thought of her.

"There's going to be at least one major solo dance," Amy supplied. "I think I'll try out. I took dance back East, you know. Tap *and* pointe." Amy had been living in Connecticut for the past few years and had moved back to her hometown of Sweet Valley just recently. Her conversation was always sprinkled with bits of trivia about things she had done "back East."

"Well, I'll tell you something I bet you don't know."

Jessica pulled the car into a parking space, and both she and Amy looked at Lila expectantly. "Well?"

Lila shrugged. "You know that girl Jade Wu? She takes dance, and I hear she's really good. I bet she'll try out."

"Jade Wu?" Amy repeated. She shook her head and glanced dubiously at Jessica. "Who is Jade Wu?"

"She's a sophomore," Jessica said. "And she's really beautiful." Opening her door, Jessica jumped out of the car, smoothed down her windblown hair. "And I've heard she's a good dancer, too. But so what? They don't give big parts to sophomores." She closed the car door.

"That's true," Lila agreed as she pushed Amy off her lap. "Protocol—juniors and seniors are supposed to be more important. Amy, you weigh about ten million pounds," she added with a petulant frown.

"Sorrreee. Let's just go to Lisette's, OK?" Amy bounced over to Jessica and squeezed her arm.

Chattering excitedly, the three girls hurried into the mall and maneuvered through the crowd toward Lisette's. The fashionable boutique catered to the wealthier, more sophisticated segment of the local population, with trendy, expensive styles and imported accessories. Lila bought most of her clothes there, and Jessica *dreamed* about buying most of her clothes there. Now she was determined to win the wardrobe.

"Look at this sweater," Lila cooed the moment they entered the shop. She pounced on a rack of tops and plucked one off as Amy wandered into the shoe department. Holding it up against her, Lila demanded, "Isn't this great? Should I try it on?"

Jessica glanced toward the sales desk, where she figured the sign-up sheet was. Three women were standing on line to make purchases, so she decided to wait. Turning back to Lila, she shrugged. "Sure. Why not?"

"Come on." With a regal wave Lila beckoned Jessica after her and headed for the dressing rooms at the back.

Following slowly, Jessica looked around the shop, calculating to herself how many new outfits she would win and which styles would look best on her. Her feet sank into the plush carpeting, and she shivered in anticipation. A whole designer wardrobe—what a luxury! She joined Lila and let out a blissful sigh.

"This is going to be so great." She noticed a line forming outside the dressing rooms. "Isn't there a room free?"

Lila grimaced and folded her arms. "No," she huffed. "I hate waiting."

At that moment the door of the dressing room directly in front of them opened, and two girls stepped out. Jessica looked up and froze. One of them was Pamela Janson.

A sly smile spread across Pamela's face. "Jennifer, right?"

"Jessica," she corrected through gritted teeth.

"Oh, right. *Jess*ica." Pamela stood firmly in the way, her smile turning nastier by the second.

Lila was staring at Jessica with impatient curiosity, and Jessica put on her most fake, insincere smile to match her rival's. "Hi, Patty—I mean, *Pam*ela," she gushed. "What a *nice* surprise." At the mention of Pamela's name, Lila's eyes widened. Jessica had told her about the incident at the beach.

"It sure is," Pamela drawled. She gave Jessica a slow, critical once-over, her eyebrows raised in surprise. "I didn't think you were the type to shop here."

"Jessica buys all her clothes here," Lila put in haughtily. She moved to Jessica's side, hands on her hips in a defiant stance.

Grateful for the support, Jessica sent Lila a silent thank-you. Obviously Lila hated Pamela on sight, too.

"Isn't that nice." Pamela's voice was frankly disbelieving, and she gave her friend a skeptical grin. "The sale rack is over there," she divulged in a mock-helpful tone. She wrinkled her nose and smiled sweetly as she turned back to Jessica and Lila.

Lila's eyes widened with indignation. "Thank you very much," she snapped.

Pamela smiled again. "You're welcome." The two Whitehead Academy girls smiled and pushed past Jessica and Lila without another word.

Jessica followed them with narrowed eyes. They stopped in front of a rack of dresses and began looking through them. For a moment Jessica was too angry to speak.

"That's her?" Lila hissed, her eyes sparking with anger. Curling her lip, she added, "She's so trashy I can't believe it."

"I know," Jessica agreed in a low, intense voice. "I can't stand her. Let's go."

"You can't let her chase you away!"

Jessica turned toward her friend, a fierce scowl on her face. "I'm not. I just can't stand breathing the same air as her. I'll throw up if I stay here much longer."

"OK, OK!"

"Let's just sign up and go. See if you can drag Amy away while I talk to the saleswoman."

Fighting down her mounting fury, Jessica hurried to the front desk and gave the saleswoman a smile. "Hi. Where do I sign up for the fashion contest?"

"Oh! Here, let me get the sheet. I'm so glad you're joining us," the saleswoman said, beaming. She fussed with some papers behind the desk.

Hurry up, hurry up, Jessica pleaded silently.

Just being in the same place with Pamela Janson made her want to scream. When she thought of the way Pamela had clamped onto A.J. at first sight, she felt like throwing a fit.

"All right, here we are. Name?"

"Jessica Wakefield."

"Size?"

Jessica tapped her foot with impatience. "Six."

"I wish I had your figure," the woman said with a laugh. "Age?"

"Sixteen."

"What's this?" came a silky voice from behind Jessica.

She turned swiftly, ready to scream. Pamela sidled up to the desk and looked at the sign-up sheet, then regarded the poster, which said, "Win a Wardrobe by Nadine—Enter the Modern Girl Fashion Show!" She smiled lazily and draped one gold-braceleted arm along the counter.

"That sounds like—fun," she said with a trace of sarcasm. She grinned at Jessica. "Are *you* signing up for this, Rebecca?"

"I thought you said Jessica," the saleswoman said. She began erasing.

"It *is* Jessica," Jessica corrected in a tight voice. She pointedly turned her back on Pamela and tried to steady her nerves. The flustered saleswoman handed her the form to complete.

"Maybe I'll sign up, too," Pamela purred. "I'd love to win a custom-designed wardrobe."

"Well, you aren't *going* to win it," Jessica retorted hotly. She looked over her shoulder for Lila and Amy. They were hurrying toward her, their faces indignant, ready for battle.

"Mmm. I think A.J. would love me in a Nadine," Pamela went on, reaching for an entry blank. She turned to her friend and let out a throaty chuckle. "He loved the dress I had on the other day. I could see by the way he never took his eyes off me. I swear, I really felt like he was undressing me!"

Jessica bit back a sharp remark. Darting her eyes up to Lila and Amy, she gave them a look that pleaded for help. Lila nodded and turned to Amy with a conspiratorial smile.

"I was talking to A.J. Morgan the other day. He said he met a girl on the beach with an ego the size of Utah," she confided in a loud whisper. Then she giggled suddenly. "And a rear end to match, too."

A spurt of triumphant laughter nearly escaped from Jessica's lips as she bent over the entry form and scribbled in her height, weight, and hair color. *All right, Lila!* she crowed silently.

"Now, girls," the clerk said, brisk and businesslike as she took their forms, "the show starts at one o'clock sharp next Saturday. The east end of the mall where they have Santa's workshop at Christmastime will be set up with a runway, curtain, and changing room."

"Can we help our friend during changes?" Amy cut in anxiously.

The woman nodded. "Of course. But keep it quiet while you're backstage. Now, depending on how many sign up, you'll have five or six outfits to model." She smiled at Jessica and Pamela. "The most important part of the show, in one respect, will be the rehearsal the night before. You *can* both make that, can't you?"

Jessica and Pamela nodded, and she went on. "Wonderful. Be here Friday at six, and we'll have a run-through without changing so you can get a feel for how it all works. You'll have a chance to see what designs you'll be modeling so you can think about your makeup for Saturday. By Friday we'll have name tags on all the designs, so you can look them over. All set on that?"

Jessica turned to glare at Pamela and said, "Fine. I'll be here."

"So will I," Pamela said emphatically, returning Jessica's glare. Leaning against the counter, she continued, "and I think I'll wear one of my new dresses when A.J. takes me to the dance at Whitehead, too. He'll like that."

Promptly Lila took Jessica by the arm and

hustled her out of the store. Amy hurried after them.

"Let me go, Lila," Jessica said, seething as Pamela's malicious laughter drifted out behind them.

"No way. I don't want to visit you in jail," her friend replied dryly.

Amy sent an outraged look over her shoulder. "That girl is incredible! What nerve! I can't believe A.J. is so gullible."

"He's not," Lila put in impatiently. She sent Jessica a knowing look. "He has much better taste than that."

"I don't know how you can be so sure," Jessica said with a glum sigh. For a moment she had to pause and collect herself. She felt surprisingly shaken up by the confrontation with Pamela. What if she *did* lose A.J. to Pamela? What would she do?

Lila shook her head. "Trust me, Jess. A.J. might be fooled for a little while, but he'd see the light pretty soon."

Jessica gave Lila a grateful hug. Lila could be a pain sometimes. But when it really counted, she was an incredibly loyal friend. "Thanks, Li. I just hope you're right."

"Believe me, I am. But that kind of girl is capable of doing *anything* to get what she wants, you know."

Amy hitched her bag up over her shoulder. "She's right, Jess. Don't trust that girl for a second. And during the show, don't worry. We'll keep an eye on her."

Startled, Jessica stopped and looked at her friends. "You don't think she'd do anything really awful to keep me from winning, do you?"

Lila shrugged expressively. "Who knows? But if she tries anything next Saturday, she'd better look out, that's all I can say."

Nine

"OK," Jeffrey said, rubbing his hands together briskly. "Here comes the big question—what do we have on our pizza? Pepperoni? Anchovies?"

Elizabeth made a face and groaned. "Anything but anchovies, please. Jess, what do you want?"

Across the table from her, Jessica shrugged and shook her head. "Oh, anything. It doesn't matter to me. Really." Then she lifted her eyes to A.J.'s face and smiled. "I'll have whatever you want."

"Well . . ." A.J. looked uncomfortable. He hitched his chair a little closer to the table as he frowned at the menu. "I like mushrooms—"

"So do I. I love mushrooms. What a good idea!" Jessica chimed in enthusiastically. "What else?"

Elizabeth felt the smile fade from her face as she listened to her twin. Going to Guido's Pizza Palace on a double date had seemed like a good idea originally. But so far, the atmosphere had been strained between the two couples. And it was because of Jessica. Elizabeth and Jeffrey both knew she wasn't being herself, and A.J. was beginning to look as though he wished he were somewhere else.

And honestly, Elizabeth thought, she couldn't blame him. No matter what he said, Jessica instantly agreed with him instead of voicing an opinion of her own. Her twin found everything A.J. said to be either witty, fascinating, or profound. With some people that kind of flattery worked, but it obviously didn't with A.J. It was clearly making him uneasy.

On top of that, she and Jeffrey were both behaving out of character, too. Elizabeth knew she was trying to compensate for her sister, and she suspected Jeffrey was doing the same. And what was worse, Jessica looked so different that Elizabeth felt strange every time she looked across the table. Jessica was wearing one of Elizabeth's favorite dresses, and her hair was pulled back the way Elizabeth's usually was. The end result was that Elizabeth really felt as though she were looking into a mirror. Usually Jessica's personality was apparent enough to make their differences obvious, but now they were like clones. It left Elizabeth feeling very unsettled. All things considered, it was far from the best double date in history.

"How about if I play something on the juke-box," Jessica suggested, smiling cheerfully.

"I'll do it," A.J. offered. He started to rise.

"No! Please, let me. Just tell me what you want, and I'll play it. Whatever you like is fine with me."

As Elizabeth watched her twin, she had to resist an urge to kick her under the table. She dropped her eyes in confusion and then met Jeffrey's bewildered glance. She gave him a tiny shrug and shook her head. She just didn't know what to do or say, or how to react to her sister.

"I'll be back in a minute. I know they changed the songs, so it'll take a while to pick out the good ones." Brimming with goodwill and sincerity, Jessica slid out from their booth and hurried away.

Jeffrey cleared his throat. "I'll go with her," he mumbled. Darting an uncertain look at Elizabeth, he scooted out and followed Jessica.

Silence descended on the table. Elizabeth's conscience was heavy, knowing she had promised Jessica not to give away the secret. She was afraid, though, that once she opened her mouth, she wouldn't be able to stop herself from blurting out the truth.

She met A.J.'s eyes and smiled, racking her brain for something to say that would sound natural. But the only thing she could think about was how seriously Jessica was ruining her chances.

"Liz?" A.J. spoke quietly, his eyes on the saltshaker he was toying with. "Is Jessica always so—I don't know—serious?" His face was tinged pink.

Elizabeth felt her heart lurch painfully. "What do you mean?" she prompted. She wished her voice didn't make it so obvious she did know what he meant.

"Always so—concerned. I'm not putting this very well," he interrupted himself. He shook his head as though to straighten out his thoughts. "It's just that with her, everything is really —important."

He stopped and cast an anguished look over his shoulder, and when he turned back to Elizabeth, his brown eyes were sad. "I'm beginning to think I'm too much of a lightweight for her. I guess I'm not really as mature as she is. I like just goofing off sometimes, but she never does."

All Elizabeth could do was look at him in silence. She had known all along this would happen, but still, it was more painful to hear than she expected. Her twin was about to get the shock of her life, and there wasn't anything

Elizabeth could do to stop it without breaking her vow. She had to stall for time.

"What do you mean?" she asked. "She's— she can be a lot of fun. You just haven't seen her, uh—lighter side yet. That's all. Really."

A.J. gulped. "I—well, I guess that's possible. I don't know. I was going to ask her to a jazz concert, but now I don't think she'd really like it very much. I get the feeling she only likes classical music."

"Oh, no. That's not true, A.J. Jessica likes all kinds of music, even rock," Elizabeth assured him. If Jessica could hear their discussion, she would have a fit.

Just tell him, her conscience urged. *Tell him what Jessica is really like. It's for Jessica's own good— she'll be heartbroken if he breaks up with her.*

"Well . . . I don't know," A.J. went on moodily. He shook his head and frowned.

"A.J.," Elizabeth began, on the verge of breaking her promise. "I think—"

"Hi. We're back."

Jessica bounced back to their booth and sat down, beaming. Jeffrey slid in next to Elizabeth without speaking and picked up his soda.

"I hope you like what we picked," Jessica said in a bright, cheerful voice. "I can't always remember who sings what, you know? I don't know much about contemporary music."

There was a choking splutter as Jeffrey coughed on his soda.

The awkward tension that had existed from the moment they sat down grew worse. Nobody looked at anybody else or spoke, except for Jessica, who kept up a bubbly chatter.

"Maybe we should order," Elizabeth said, her tone grim. She picked up her menu and studied it intently. As far as she was concerned, the evening couldn't end soon enough. It was already a disaster, and it could only go downhill from then on.

"You were sure acting strange tonight, Liz." Jessica strolled into Elizabeth's bedroom, hairbrush in hand, and sat down on her twin's bed.

Elizabeth was at her desk, writing in her journal, but she stopped when Jessica spoke. Without looking up, she asked, "What do you mean?"

"I don't know. Strange. Like you were upset about something." Jessica leaned back on one elbow and crossed her ankles. "Is something bugging you?"

"Jess—" Elizabeth turned in her chair and gave her a bewildered look. Then she let her breath out slowly and asked, "Did you have fun tonight? With A.J.?"

Jessica kept her smile in place, but inside, she

110

was fighting a growing sense of panic. She knew something was wrong, but she couldn't even admit it to herself, let alone to her twin. "Yeah, sure. I mean, it wasn't our greatest date of all time, but I'm happy just being with him."

There was a tense silence for a few moments. Jessica kept her eyes on her feet because she sensed her sister was struggling for words.

At last Elizabeth slapped her pen down on the desk and crossed to Jessica's side. Elizabeth sat on the bed and looked into her sister's eyes soberly. "Jess. Please, *please* stop acting that way around A.J."

"What way?" Jessica prompted, her cheeks warming.

"You know. Spineless. Weak—like a complete airhead! You're going to lose him if you keep it up."

Jessica swallowed hard. She met her twin's eyes and said, "I'm only acting the way you do."

A look of complete surprise crossed Elizabeth's face. Her mouth dropped open. "What?"

Feeling both exasperated and embarrassed, Jessica rolled away from her sister, onto her stomach. "A.J. likes all the kinds of things you do. You know—books, nature, taking a stand on issues."

"You haven't taken a stand on anything in weeks!" Elizabeth retorted vehemently.

Jessica kept her face down, and she could feel her cheeks burning. *This whole thing is such a disaster!* she moaned inwardly. *Why can't I do anything right?*

"And besides, is that how you think I am? The way you've been acting lately?" Elizabeth's voice rose in pitch. "I can't believe you think of me that way! You really think I'm such a wimp?"

"I don't—I mean, you're not—I don't know!" Tears sprang to Jessica's eyes, and she sniffed, feeling miserable.

"Jessica! You can be nice without being a wimp, you know. I don't go around acting like a doormat! I just—" Elizabeth broke off and let out a frustrated sigh. "Listen, Jess. I don't know why you think acting like me will make A.J. like you better. He doesn't like *me*—you're the one he asked out."

"Only because he thought I was like you," Jessica insisted. She rubbed her thumb along the bristles of her hairbrush, feeling completely dejected.

Another weighty silence fell. Jessica knew her sister was looking at her, waiting, maybe even trying to tell her something.

"Well, is it working?" Elizabeth asked finally, her voice low and grave.

A sob of pain welled up in Jessica's throat. Everything in front of her blurred as tears flooded her eyes. "No. It's not."

112

"Then why won't you stop?"

Frantic, Jessica shook her head. "Because it's too late to change. What would A.J. think now if he found out I'm not really like this? He'd drop me in a minute. I know I can make it work, Liz."

With tears slipping down her cheeks, Jessica pushed herself up off the bed and shook her head. "It's the only thing I can do," she said mechanically. All she could do was cling stubbornly to her original plan. She was positive that backing out now would only make things worse than they already were.

Sunk in gloom, she gave her twin one last unhappy look and plodded back to her own room.

Elizabeth watched her sister drag herself away. The look of pain and misery on Jessica's face was almost more than Elizabeth could stand. Part of her wished she had had the nerve to come right out and tell Jessica what A.J. had said at Guido's. Hearing the blunt, unvarnished truth—that A.J. was turned off by Jessica's attitude—might finally do the trick. But it was also possible that knowing A.J. wasn't interested anymore could break Jessica's heart.

"What should I do?" Elizabeth whispered anxiously. Taking a deep breath, she sat back down at her desk and picked up her pen. She reread the last few lines of her journal.

I think she could tell how bad things were, but I'm not sure. She acts so perky and smiles so much now, it's hard to tell what's really going on inside. It's like I don't even know her.

Deep in thought, Elizabeth bent over her journal and continued.

I just wish there was something I could do to help her. I know how horrible she must feel, and it kills me to see her so depressed. If I were Jessica—the old Jessica— I'd do something really sneaky to straighten things out. The old Jessica would try any scheme if she thought it would work. Anonymous letters, starting rumors, manipulating people . . .

Elizabeth paused and looked back over what she had written. She was torn by conflicting emotions. Describing Jessica's devious ways brought on a wave of nostalgia. Sneaky, manipulative, scheming—she loved and missed that Jessica so much!

Yet at the same time, she knew she couldn't use any of her sister's tricks, and not just because they usually backfired. It didn't work when Jessica acted like her, and it wouldn't work if she tried to act like Jessica. Trying to be someone else was always a mistake, even if it was for the best of reasons.

Her shoulders sagged as she sat staring into space. She didn't know how the situation could end happily. It looked impossible now.

"Oh, Jess," she said with a sigh, shaking her head. "I'm so sorry."

Ten

On Monday at lunch Jessica threw herself into a chair across from Cara, Amy, and Lila and sullenly snapped open a can of diet soda. She took a long drink, refusing to meet her friends' curious looks. She didn't feel very much like talking. All around them, the cafeteria was buzzing with laughter and conversation. Everyone in the world seemed to be in a good mood. Except for her.

"Where's A.J.?" Amy piped up. "Aren't you guys eating lunch together?"

Giving her friend a resentful glance, Jessica propped her chin up on her fist. "He had a teacher conference or something," she grumbled in a peevish tone. She pushed her soda can back and forth through a puddle of condensation on the table.

"Been to any good committee meetings lately?" Lila asked.

A snort of laughter escaped from Cara. She hastily clamped one hand over her mouth and buried her face in her slam book.

"Lila, give me a break, OK?"

"Just asking," her friend said. Grinning impishly, she went on, "It's just that I saw a nuclear freeze poster, and I was wondering if you made it."

"Ha, ha, ha." Jessica put as much scorn into her voice as she could muster, but she didn't really feel like battling with Lila at the moment.

Lila tossed her light brown hair over her shoulders and leaned across the table. Her brown eyes were alive with curiosity. "So, what did A.J. say when you told him about the fashion contest?"

Jessica conjured up a mental picture of A.J. at Guido's. It had seemed like nothing she could say sparked his interest. He had been polite, of course. He was always polite. But he didn't really seem to care one way or the other how many fashion contests she entered. The truth was, he seemed to be indifferent to everything she said or did now. It was only a matter of time before he broke up with her, she realized frantically. And she didn't know how to keep him.

She made an attempt at a nonchalant shrug. "He said it was great. He said he's really excited about it." The frank disbelief in Lila's eyes made Jessica feel uncomfortable.

"Really?" Amy pushed. She pursed her lips in a thoughtful pout. "So he's going, right?"

"Yeah."

"How about you?"

Jessica's head snapped up at Cara's question. She narrowed her eyes. "What?"

Glancing at Lila, Cara said, "Just asking if you'll be there, too. The real Jessica."

An angry retort sprang to Jessica's lips. But she was so conditioned *not* to say anything mean that she stopped herself and just looked away. It was getting so she couldn't be herself at all anymore, even around her friends.

"Lay off, OK? Please?" she said.

"OK," Cara murmured. "Just don't be surprised if we have to put a new category in the slam books."

Jessica darted a suspicious look across the table at her friend. She knew she shouldn't ask, but she couldn't help it. "What?"

"Most Schizophrenic?" Cara suggested. She smiled mischievously and then quickly shook her head. "Just kidding, Jess. Honest."

Stung, Jessica looked away from Cara. Everybody was after her, trying to sabotage her plan to win A.J. Elizabeth, her friends, everyone. It just wasn't fair. She couldn't seem to make anyone understand that keeping up her act was the *only* way. A.J. wouldn't like the real Jessica, she was convinced of it.

"She didn't mean it," Amy put in, seeing Jessica's discomfort.

"It was just a joke, Jess, really," Cara said earnestly. "A dumb joke. I shouldn't have even said it. I'm sorry."

"I don't know," Lila said. She examined Jessica critically and went on in her typically blunt manner. "I think you're turning into the bore of the century, if you want my opinion."

"Well, I don't, OK? Keep your opinions to yourself." Jessica scraped her chair back and stood up, fighting the urge to burst into tears. She stared at her three best friends for a moment and then stormed off, pushing her way through the maze of crowded tables.

Her friends watched her in silence. Finally Cara looked at Amy and Lila. "Think we hurt her feelings?" she asked in a worried tone.

Amy puffed out her cheeks and shook her head. "Yeah. But even that didn't work."

"We have to think of something else." Lila jangled her gold bracelets and let out a frustrated sigh.

"Yeah," Cara agreed. "But what?"

Amy looked thoughtful as she munched on a carrot stick. "I don't know," she said. "I really thought ganging up on her would work." She looked at Lila, and seeing the expression on her friend's face, Amy sat up straighter in her chair. "Do you have a better idea, Lila?"

"I might," Lila answered. Narrowing her eyes, she folded her arms across her chest and thought. The three of them had been racking their brains, trying to find a way to get Jessica to snap out of her act. If telling her she was boring hadn't worked, Lila didn't know what would. Then a picture of Pamela Janson sprang to her mind.

"That girl. Pamela."

"Huh?" Cara raised her eyebrows. "What about her?"

Lila rolled her eyes. "Look. If Jessica wants something bad enough—and if someone tries to take it away from her—"

"She'll fight back," Amy concluded triumphantly. Then her face fell. "But what can we do about it? We can't make Pamela do anything we want."

Lila chuckled and shook her head. "That's just it. If we're lucky, she'll do it all by herself, and we won't have to do a thing."

"A.J.? Telephone!"

Mrs. Morgan's voice drifted into A.J.'s room on Wednesday night. He dropped the play he was reading for English and pushed himself off his bed. "I'll get it in your room, Mom!" he called.

He hurried down the hallway to his parents' bedroom and picked up the phone by the bed. "Hello?"

"Hi, A.J. It's me, Pamela Janson."

A.J. felt a wave of excitement wash over him at the sound of her voice. He smiled nervously. "Hi. How's it going?"

"*Awful.* I'm so bored. I have off from school for a week, and I'm stuck at home with *nothing* to do."

To A.J. it sounded as if she were pouting. He could picture her perfectly—that alluring smile, those sultry blue eyes, those long tanned legs. But half of him still resisted the impulse to respond the way he knew he could.

"Oh, too bad," he replied, trying to keep his tone light. He cradled the receiver against his ear and leaned back on one elbow. "Maybe you should have a hobby."

Pamela's rich, throaty laugh rippled over the line. "But I *do* have a hobby, A.J. Or at least, I'm working on one."

"What do you mean?"

"You know exactly what I mean," she purred.

A.J. nodded, his eyes fixed on the telephone. He did know what she meant. He had never thought he'd be attracted to someone as aggressive and seductive as Pamela was. That style had always seemed like such a turnoff before. In the past he had always preferred shy, quiet girls like Jessica. But for some reason, with Jessica, he was getting more shyness and quiet than he really wanted. Now he found himself wishing he could be with Pamela instead. She was like the car she drove—fast, sleek, exciting, and dangerous.

"So are you coming to the dance at Whitehead with me?" she went on in her low, silky voice. "I'll die of humiliation if you stand me up now. I told everyone you'd be there."

A jolt of alarm brought A.J. back to reality, and he sat bolt upright on the bed. He had to keep reminding himself he was still going out with Jessica. He couldn't make any commitments to Pamela until—unless—that changed.

"Listen, Pamela. I'd really like to say yes," he faltered, rubbing one palm on a knee. "But I'm not sure I can. I can't explain it—"

"You're not still going out with that dishrag, are you?"

A.J.'s cheeks burned. "Pamela, I—"

"Oh, no! I'm so awful, I can't believe I said that!" she interrupted with a silvery laugh. She groaned dramatically. "I'm sorry. Forget it. Now I *really* feel like a witch."

"No, it's OK," A.J. hastened to assure her. "Don't worry about it."

"Well, are you sure you're not mad at me? You don't hate me, do you?"

"No, Pamela. Forget it. It's OK. And I definitely don't hate you."

In the back of A.J.'s mind, he realized he was apologizing to Pamela because she had insulted Jessica. That triggered a skeptical reaction, but he shook it off impatiently.

Pamela let out a sigh. "OK. Listen, I have to go—promise you'll think about that dance. And you'll give me your answer at the fashion show on Saturday, OK? I assume you'll be going to see your *friend* in it, right? I've entered it, too. See you then."

"I'll—"

She hung up before he could respond. A.J. slowly replaced the receiver and sat staring into space.

Who do I really like? he asked himself moodily. *Jessica or Pamela?*

* * *

Elizabeth backed through the newspaper office door on Thursday afternoon, her arms laden with books and papers. She let out a sigh of relief as she set them down.

"Are you in training or something, Liz?" Olivia Davidson asked. Olivia was the arts editor of *The Oracle*, and she spent long hours at the office working on features.

"Not quite." Elizabeth grinned wryly and began sorting through her papers. "Got anything good for my column, Liv?"

"Mmm. I don't know. How about the auditions for the music and dance show?"

As she took a seat at one of the typewriters, Elizabeth smiled. "Inspiration. I can fill up at least one whole paragraph wondering who's going to try out."

Olivia laughed and bent her head over her work again, and Elizabeth rolled a sheet of paper into the typewriter. "I must be really out of it today. After all, I *am* doing the p.r. for the show. 'Eyes and Ears' is a perfect place to mention it."

She began tapping away at the keys. As she speculated on who might audition, obvious choices sprang to mind. But when it was time to toss around names for the main dancing role, she drew a blank.

"Liv? Who would you say is the best dancer at school that you know of?"

Olivia looked thoughtful as she twirled her pencil between two fingers. "I'd have to say Jade Wu. I saw her at her ballet class once when I was doing a story about studying dance."

"Jade Wu?" Elizabeth echoed. The petite, black-haired sophomore was shy and quiet, and Elizabeth only knew her by sight. "Hmm. I didn't realize . . ."

"She's never been in a show at school, so far. I don't know why," Olivia continued. She shrugged matter-of-factly. "So I don't know if she's even interested in trying out, but you could put her down."

Elizabeth nodded. "OK, thanks. I will."

Elizabeth was concentrating on her article when there was a knock on the door. She looked up expectantly and blinked in surprise when Lila Fowler stuck her head into the office.

"Liz, can I talk to you a second?"

"Sure, Lila." Elizabeth tried not to look too startled. As a rule, she and Lila didn't have much to say to each other. She pushed her chair back and crossed to the door. "What's up?"

Lila beckoned her out into the empty hallway. Without introduction she began, "I'm worried about Jessica, and I know you are, too."

Frowning, Elizabeth nodded. "So . . . ?"

"So, I've been thinking. I have an idea about how to get her back to normal."

"How?" Elizabeth looked at her sister's friend, a look of guarded hope in her eyes.

Lila gave her an offhand nod. "Talk about Pamela."

"Pamela?"

"Yes, Pamela!" Letting out an exasperated sigh, Lila shifted her feet and faced Elizabeth squarely. "Look. The only way she's going to act like herself is if she has to fight for A.J., OK? Trust me on this one."

Elizabeth had to fight back a sarcastic remark about trusting Lila. In the past, it hadn't always been a very good policy to follow. Lila's plans were calculated to serve Lila's interests. A prime example was the Couples of the Future mix-up in which Elizabeth had been paired with A.J.: that had been Lila's work, for her own devious motives. And Elizabeth was still stinging from the incident. But this time maybe Jessica's friend was right, Elizabeth thought. She gave Lila a cautious nod.

"OK," she agreed, her voice hesitant. "Just talk about Pamela?"

Lila smiled a slow feline smile. "That's right. I want her ready to fight on Saturday, got it?"

Full understanding dawned on Elizabeth. She pictured her twin fighting mad, going all out for what she wanted. That was the real Jessica.

"And Friday night—the rehearsal—is the time to hit her hardest."

Elizabeth nodded again and gave Lila a grudgingly appreciative look. "OK, Lila. You're on."

"These are really great," Jessica bubbled, examining the clothes with "J. Wakefield" on the name tags. It was Friday evening, and she and Lila and Amy were at the mall, waiting for the fashion show rehearsal to start. Half a dozen other girls were milling around, eagerly looking over the Nadine designs on the racks.

"Mmm. The blue one especially," Lila agreed.

Jessica's eyes shone with excitement. "It'll look great on me, I know it."

"I bet it would look good on someone like Pamela, too," Amy put in.

Irritated, Jessica looked at Amy and gave her an angry scowl. "Whose side are you on, anyway?"

"I was just saying—"

"Oh, forget it," Lila interrupted impatiently. "Pamela's going to look good in whatever she has on, so what difference does it make if she'd look good in this?"

Jessica stared at her friends, flabbergasted. They had been talking about Pamela nonstop—how pretty she was, what a great car she drove. And they were constantly nagging *her* about how she should act, how she should dress, what she should say. She thought if she heard the name Pamela one more time she would explode.

Frowning, Jessica turned away and was just in time to see Pamela herself walk in. She narrowed her eyes and followed the girl's entrance. If there was one person in the world she would be happy to see fall flat on her face on the runway, it was Pamela Janson.

"OK, girls," called the Lisette's saleswoman. She strode forward with a clipboard in her hand. "When I call your name, come forward and line up, please."

"Hey, did you just see Pamela come in?" Lila asked casually.

Jessica whirled around on her friend. "Yes, I did," she said in a tight voice. "*Thanks* for pointing it out to me, Lila."

"You're welcome." Lila smiled innocently and gave her a nudge. "They just called your name, Jess. Go for it."

Restraining a bitter retort, Jessica turned and stalked away. If she got through the rehearsal without screaming her head off, she'd consider herself lucky.

Eleven

Jessica's heart was fluttering wildly as she, Lila, and Amy hurried into the mall the next day. She was so nervous she couldn't even look at her friends, let alone talk. They were chattering on without her, oblivious of her inner turmoil.

Something told Jessica that everything would be decided at the fashion show once and for all. A.J. would have a chance to see her and Pamela side by side, and she was horribly afraid Pamela would outshine her. How could she hope to compete, when Pamela had no qualms about showing off and making herself look dazzling? And Jessica was stuck with her meek and mousy masquerade. If she only dared, she would put herself into high gear and give it everything she had. But that would be the side of her she hadn't let A.J. see—and she was too worried about their relationship to put it to the test.

"Hurry up, Jess! I bet Pamela's already here!" Lila's words reached her ears, taunting her.

How did I ever get into this mess? Jessica asked herself desperately as they wove through the noontime crowd.

And why does everyone keep talking about that stupid Pamela?

Between Lila and Amy and Elizabeth, she had been hearing about nothing but Pamela Janson for two days straight. She didn't know what had gotten into them, but she was ready to kill them as well as Pamela. She had nearly lost control the night before at the run-through, but she had managed to keep cool with tremendous effort.

"Come on, Jess. This way." Lila and Amy waved her on, heading for the end of the mall where the fashion show was to take place.

Ahead, Jessica saw the modeling runway on which she had practiced walking. It was surrounded by rows and rows of chairs, and the seats were already beginning to fill up. She felt a prickle of nerves as she recognized dozens of Sweet Valley High students. Not wanting to make eye contact with anybody, she kept her face down and followed Lila and Amy.

Behind the runway a heavy velvet curtain hid the makeshift backstage area. They ducked behind the curtain and entered a noisy beehive of activity. Girls and women were rushing back and forth, chattering, putting on makeup, and trying on Nadine's stylish clothes.

Jessica looked around the area and saw Pamela Janson. As though sensing her hostile gaze, Pamela looked up and grinned slyly as their eyes met. The smile sent a quiver of hot anger through Jessica. She fumed and turned to her friends.

"Come on. Let's get started."

"Are you girls all competing?" The saleswoman from Lisette's came bustling toward them, clipboard in hand.

"I am, and my friends are helping me change," Jessica said. Lila and Amy moved closer to her and nodded.

"Oh, of course. You're Jessica. I remember you."

The woman gave them a preoccupied smile and gestured vaguely over her shoulder. "OK, you know what to do. Have fun."

Jessica, Lila, and Amy exchanged a determined look and headed for the clothes racks. Girls were flitting back and forth all around them, checking themselves in mirrors and making adjustments to their clothes. It was a chaotic atmosphere. There were twelve contestants altogether, plus their friends, mothers, and helpers, in addition to all the people who were there to run the show.

Trying hard to concentrate amid the hectic noise and activity, Jessica hurried to the racks and snapped impatiently through the hangers. The blue dress she had admired the night before was her first outfit, and she rapidly slipped it off the hanger.

"This is definitely my best color," she said confidently. She began unbuttoning her blouse, and Lila and Amy emptied Lila's enormous makeup bag onto a nearby table. They had brought their combined makeup inventory.

"I'm going to look outside," Amy said. "I'll be right back."

"Jess, Nadine is here," hissed Lila. She jerked her head toward the other side of the room. "That's her in the red flight-suit thing."

For a moment Jessica paused in her undressing and sent an apprehensive look across the room. The designer was calling out orders like a glamorous drill sergeant, gesturing and pointing and shaking her head. Nadine herself would pick the winner, and of course she was the one who would design the prize wardrobe. Jessica felt a wild impulse to throw herself at Nadine's feet and beg for her vote. She wasn't sure she could win on her own.

Amy came hurrying back, her eyes wide with excitement. "Everyone's here," she gasped, snatching up a hairbrush. "*Everyone.*"

"Five minutes, girls!" Nadine called out.

Jessica bit her lower lip and stepped into her first outfit. It was a clingy, nubby knit dress in light blue cotton. As she smoothed the sleeves down her arms, she had to admire the way the dress showed off her figure. It was skintight, with a wide, off-the-shoulder neckline. Amy scurried around behind Jessica and began brushing her hair with swift strokes.

"Not so hard, Amy. Ow!"

Jessica winced, and Lila descended upon her with a huge makeup brush.

"Your blush is a total mess," Lila said succinctly.

Closing her eyes, Jessica let her friends hover around her, perfecting and polishing her image. She tried to steady her racing pulse and felt an almost irresistible urge to look for Pamela. She peeked through her lashes, scanning the room for her arch enemy. The girl was nowhere in sight.

Beyond the curtain a driving rock beat started up. The tension in the dressing area instantly grew more electric. Jessica's heart gave a wild jump, and she stepped into the blue pumps that went with her dress. "Wish me luck, you guys," she muttered.

Her friends nodded and gave her a professional review. "You look great," Lila said in a businesslike tone. She smoothed Jessica's hair into place. "Go get on line."

Nodding quickly, Jessica hurried to the curtain, where the other contestants were forming a line. They had memorized the order the night before. Jessica threw a nervous smile back at her friends.

All the other girls looked edgy and excited, and Nadine herself, standing to one side, kept up a low murmur of last-minute instructions. As Jessica took her place, she sensed someone rushing up behind her. Just then she felt the person bump into her from behind and let out a startled exclamation.

"Oh, no! My bracelet is caught on your dress!" Pamela's voice brought Jessica around with a start. At the same time she felt a pulling sensation up the back of her dress.

"What are you doing!" she hissed. Applause from the audience came clamoring through the curtain as the first girl went out.

Pamela was yanking at a gold chain around

her wrist. The clasp was snapped in the nubby fabric of Jessica's dress. "Gee, I'm so sorry," Pamela gushed, pulling harder and dragging on the caught yarn.

Craning her head around, Jessica saw a huge pull up the back of the dress: the hemline was rucked up where the yarn had been dragged through, and a huge loop of yarn was hanging down the back. Anger surged through her. "Oh, no! Look what you *did*!"

"I'm so sorry," Pamela repeated as she backed up. She snapped off the thread with a vicious yank. Her eyes sparkled with malicious laughter, and she shook her head. "I wonder if it's ruined."

"I—"

"You're on!"

Pamela gave her a quick shove through the gap in the curtain, and Jessica stumbled out onto the runway. A blaze of lights nearly blinded her, but she kept her head lifted high and walked forward to a round of applause.

Just keep walking, keep smiling, don't let them see how furious you are, she commanded herself sternly.

Inside, though, she was livid. Pamela had deliberately snagged her dress, she was sure of it. But all she could do was smile. Through the lights, she could just barely make out the faces of people in the crowd: her twin, sitting with Cara and Steven and their parents, and A.J., sitting with some Sweet Valley boys. A jolt of panic swept through her. Everyone was going to see how ridiculous her dress looked when she turned around.

"Jessica is wearing an off-the-shoulder knit, mid-thigh and very formfitting," the announcer's voice crooned over the music just as Jessica reached the end of the runway. "Perfect for parties and special evenings on the town."

Jessica thought fast. If she turned around to walk back, everyone would see. Instead, she took her cue from the rock music and began dancing—sashaying and skipping and rocking backward up the runway while she smiled brightly at the audience. There was no time to wonder if she was keeping up her Elizabeth act. There was no time to worry what A.J. thought of her. She had to pull off a good show, no matter what. A round of applause broke out and she heard a cheer from some of her friends.

"Go, Jessica!"

"Looking good, Wakefield!"

Her heart racing, she backed through the opening in the curtain with her dazzling smile still cemented in place. Once inside, she turned in fury on Pamela Janson.

"Nice trick," she hissed as Pamela brushed past her. "But it didn't work."

Pamela gave her a haughty glance. "I don't know what you're talking about."

"Sure." Jessica narrowed her eyes in anger, and Pamela disappeared through the gap. Then Lila and Amy tugged her arms and hustled her back for her next change.

"It's the denim dress—really tight," Amy explained breathlessly.

Lila helped Jessica off with the knit dress and draped it over one arm. "We saw what she did, that sneak."

"Yeah, well, she can't do it with denim, at least." Jessica's voice was grim as she slipped the dress on over her head. Two zippers ran up the sides of the dress to make it as skintight as possible. She tugged hastily at the right one, and it jammed.

"Oh, no!" she groaned, scowling ferociously. She struggled to free it. "Somebody get the other side! Hurry!"

Lila's fingers fumbled at her other side while Jessica wrestled with her zipper.

"It's stuck—it won't go!" Lila gasped.

For a moment Jessica had to close her eyes in order to calm down. She could feel Amy and Lila at her sides, examining the two zippers.

"Some of these teeth have been twisted—look at this!" came Amy's outraged voice.

"And this one," Lila chimed in. "Jess, Pamela must've done this. It's sabotage."

Jessica's eyes flew open. There was no time to lose. The dress gaped open at her sides, but she grabbed a wide leather belt from a nearby table and cinched it tight at her waist. Above and below the belt, two gaps showed through at each side, but in a daring, stylish way. It looked as though it was supposed to be that way. She grabbed the Australian outback hat that matched the outfit and raced for the curtain. There was no way she would let Pamela ruin her chances.

"Here's Jessica again, in our outback dress—perfect for rough wear without sacrificing style!"

Smiling, Jessica strolled down the runway, swinging her hat from one hand in debonair nonchalance. The lights, the music, the audience all combined to drive her on down the runway. She was in her element. She *had* to succeed.

When she reached the end, she paused, looked at the audience, and winked. The gaps at her waist showed clearly as she raised her arms above her head. Cheers and applause greeted her as she set the hat on her head at a rakish angle, turned, and sauntered back. Someone whistled in admiration, and she sent Pamela a sardonic smile as they passed each other.

"Strike two."

Pamela gave her a malevolent glare but didn't say anything. Not wasting any more time, Jessica ran back to change her clothes again.

"You're not going to believe this," Lila announced, her voice steely. "We checked all your clothes, and they've almost all been sabotaged."

Jessica stared at her. "You're kidding. I can't *believe* she would stoop so low."

"Believe it," Amy said grimly. "She must've come early just so she could do it. Come on, Jess. You've got to change."

In cold, icy fury, Jessica unhooked the belt from around her waist and got back to work. Pamela wasn't going to get away with it. There was no way she'd let that happen.

"She only has two more after this," Amy breathed, wincing anxiously.

Lila nodded, deep in thought. "I know. I know." She glanced over to where Pamela and two other Whitehead girls were changing clothes. There had to be something she and Amy could do to salvage Jessica's chances of winning. Revenge could come later, but for now, Lila knew she had to think fast. Rock music and applause drifted in from beyond the curtain while she stood stock-still.

"Amy! Lila!"

Lila whirled around at the sound of Elizabeth's voice. "What are you doing here?"

Elizabeth was wearing a puzzled frown. She hurried toward them. "Is something weird going on? What's wrong with Jess?"

"Does it show?" Amy gasped. She sent Lila an anguished look. "Oh, no. I thought she could pull it off."

Elizabeth shook her head. "She looks great, but I can tell she's upset about something." She looked from Lila to Amy and back again. "Is it Pamela?" she demanded astutely.

"Yeah." In a few short words Lila filled Elizabeth in on the sabotage. "But Jessica's doing the best she can with what she's got, that's all I can say."

"Well, she does look great. I think I'm the only one who can tell something's wrong," Elizabeth said with a frustrated sigh. She shook her head. "That Pamela is too much."

"Don't worry about her," Lila replied in a mild, quiet undertone. She slid her glance across the room to the Whitehead girls. "She'll get what's coming to her."

Elizabeth gave her a startled, suspicious look.

142

"You aren't going to do anything, are you? I don't want Jess to be embarrassed anymore or get in some kind of trouble."

"No, of course not." Lila shook her head vehemently. "I just meant that these things have a way of backfiring, that's all. Really."

Amy nodded quickly and Lila went on. "And besides, Jess is so mad now, she'll probably take care of it herself." She smiled innocently and gave Jessica's twin a friendly little shove. "Now, go on. Go on back out so you can watch Jessica's last two turns. You don't want to miss her."

Reluctantly Elizabeth nodded and walked away. Silent and thoughtful, Lila and Amy watched her go.

"You're planning something," Amy said when Elizabeth was out of earshot. She gave Lila a questioning glance.

"Well . . . I don't know what, but we have to do something. Jess needs our help. She *might* be able to take care of things on her own, but just to make sure. . . ." Lila looked around the bustling changing room in contemplative silence.

"Lila?"

She sent Amy a slow, knowing smile. "You have to fight fire with fire, Amy. Now, let's figure out how to put a match under that trashy Pamela Janson."

Twelve

Jessica maneuvered back to Amy and Lila, shrugging out of her top as she ran. "Last one, right?" she said with a breathless gasp. Her pulse was still racing with the sound of applause and the thrill of parading down the runway.

"Yeah. It's the bathing suit and cover-up from the resort wear collection," Amy reminded her. "And it's OK, too. Pamela must not have had time to do anything to it."

Lila held her hands out for the clothes Jessica was shucking. "Just one more, Jess. Keep it up. You're doing great."

"Mmm . . ." Darting a quick, apprehensive glance across the room, Jessica fought back a feeling of impending disaster and put on the bathing suit. Pamela had one chance left to do something really awful to her. But Jessica swore to herself she wouldn't give the girl the satisfaction. She might not be able to win the contest, but Pamela definitely couldn't make her fall to pieces.

All around them the other contestants were changing into bikinis and tank suits, shorts and halter tops. Jessica felt goose bumps along her arms as she waited, wondering when and if Pamela was going to strike. She frowned as she pushed her arms into a filmy, semitransparent robe. Amy put a necklace of clicking seashells around her neck.

"Give me that hairbrush," she whispered, her eyes scanning the crowded room.

Lila brushed Jessica's hair for her, arranging it around her shoulders. "Just relax. We're watching out for her. She can't get you."

"I sure hope not," Jessica muttered. She was tense with anticipation. She was sure Pamela was plotting some final blow.

"What if she does something in front of A.J.?"

Lila and Amy shared a look, and then Lila shrugged. "Then he'll know what she's really like, right?"

Jessica's stomach fluttered. She hugged her

flimsy wrap around her and tried to calm herself down. So far she hadn't had time to wonder what A.J. was thinking about the whole production. She hadn't exactly been modest and conservative when she was strutting down the runway. All she had been able to concentrate on was putting on a good show in spite of Pamela's sabotage. She couldn't do that *and* keep up her sweet act at the same time. But she didn't want to think about that now. Pamela and her potential dirty tricks were too much on her mind.

"Girls! On line please for beachwear!"

"This is it, Jess. Go for it." Amy's eyes were shining, and she squeezed Jessica's hand for good luck.

With a preoccupied nod Jessica hurried back toward the curtain to wait her turn to make a final entrance. From the corner of her eye, she saw Pamela and her Whitehead cronies standing to one side, passing around a big paper cup. Jessica wished momentarily that Lila and Amy had thought to bring some sodas, but she turned away and waited for her cue. She and Pamela were among the last three girls to go out.

"Jessica?"

She turned quickly at the sound of Pamela's

voice. The girl was walking toward her, her hand outstretched with the big cup.

"Want some?" With a big smile on her face, Pamela came forward. "It's ice water."

All Jessica's instincts told her not to trust the offer. Shaking her head, she backed up just as Pamela tripped dramatically and flung her arms up. The full cup came flying toward Jessica, who ducked with a shriek. Too late, she felt the shock of ice water hitting her full in the face and chest.

"Oh, Jessica! I'm *sorry*." Pamela's voice oozed insincerity.

Jessica held her arms very still at her side. Ice-cold water dripped down her entire body, and her filmy beach wrap clung to her in huge wet patches. For the moment all she could think about was all the times in the past few weeks when she'd wanted to speak out and hadn't. She was through with playing the sweet, understanding type. This was all-out war.

Drawing a deep breath, Jessica said, "That's *it*, Janson. I'm sick and tired of you trying to ruin everything I care about, you hear me!"

Pamela raised one eyebrow. "It was an accident. I don't know what you're talking about."

"Oh, yes you do. But you know what? It

doesn't bother me because I realize you're only doing it out of jealousy!"

"Give me a break, Jessica," the girl scoffed.

"Give you a break? Are you kidding? I've given you every break there is, and you *still* can't get what you want without sneaky, dirty tricks! And you know what else? I think you helped me out today, too! You thought I'd fall apart when my clothes did, didn't you? Well, sorry, Pamela. I still looked better than you did."

"That's not true!" Pamela gasped, her eyes huge with indignation. Her voice rose, and she clenched her fists at her sides. "You looked like a total fool. Everyone was laughing at you. Especially A.J."

Jessica laughed, feeling freer and more in command than she had in a long time. "You *wish*, Pamela. You wish. You're pathetic, you know that? You can't get a guy on your own, so you have to steal other girls', right? And use cheap tricks to do it, too. Well, for your information, Pamela, A.J. isn't that stupid."

"That's what you think!"

Out in the audience a ripple of uneasy murmurs swept through the crowd. The girls already on the runway looked at each other uncertainly. Angry voices could be heard from behind the curtain. Every word came through loud and clear. No one missed a syllable.

"That's Jess," Elizabeth said in a horrified whisper. She looked at Cara and Steven with wide eyes. They nodded mutely. Her heart beating quickly, Elizabeth started to rise. All she could think of was that her sister needed her help.

"Wait, Liz!" Cara grabbed her arm and held her in her seat. Her wide, dark eyes were fixed on the runway.

As Elizabeth—and everybody else—watched in stupefied silence, the curtain began parting slowly to reveal Jessica and Pamela. They were arguing so heatedly, they seemed oblivious of the audience they now had.

"You deliberately ruined every one of my dresses," Jessica shouted, hands on her hips. "You jammed the zippers, ripped the hems, and poured water on me. I wasn't going to tell anybody because I didn't want to stoop to your level! And besides, I can look good in anything, Pamela Janson. Thanks for helping me prove it!"

Elizabeth felt her mouth drop open as she took in the scene. It was the old Jessica up there on the stage, and she hadn't looked so fantastic in weeks. Drops of water glittered in her hair like diamonds, bouncing a halo of rainbows all around her every time she moved her head. She seemed to be surrounded by stars. And the sexy, clingy beach outfit she was wearing showed off every curve of her body. She looked absolutely stunning.

Beside her, Pamela looked small and insignificant. She kept trying to get a word in edgewise, but Jessica wouldn't let her. "I hope everyone hears about this, Pamela. Because when they do, you are going to get into so much trouble, you won't know what hit you. And thanks for doing me a favor, too. Now, I know I've been acting like a pushover, but forget it! You can't push me around, Janson. So don't even try."

With that, she whirled around to head for the runway. Her look of righteous indignation froze as she realized she was in plain view, and at the same instant Pamela turned her head. For a moment there was total silence.

Then someone in the audience started clapping, and in a moment others joined in. Soon a deafening round of applause and shouts of "Go, Jess!" filled the air. Pamela stood stone still for a moment, then burst into tears and fled.

"I can't believe it," Elizabeth gasped, nearly paralyzed by shock. She swallowed hard. "I can't believe it."

Up on stage, Jessica took in the applause, and a wide smile gradually broke over her face. With a dignified flourish she caught up the trailing ends of her soaking wet beach wrap and took a deep bow. She was dazzling, and the applause doubled in volume.

"Ladies and gentlemen! Attention, please!" Nadine stepped forward onto the runway, microphone in hand, and gestured for silence. The thunderous applause continued for another moment and then settled down.

Nadine beckoned to Jessica with one hand. "In keeping with the theme of this fashion show, I think it's obvious that the winner is standing next to me now!" she announced with a broad smile. "Here's a girl who knows what she wants and goes for it with everything she's got!"

The audience broke into another round of applause, and the Sweet Valley High boys started stomping their feet in rhythm. "JESS-I-CA! JESS-I-CA!" they chanted.

Elizabeth laughed out loud and shook her head. "You're really something, Jess," she murmured under her breath. "You are really something else."

* * *

"And since it was so obvious that Pamela was cheating like crazy," Jessica chattered happily, "she was instantly disqualified. She'll never show her face in Sweet Valley again."

Smiling in satisfaction, Jessica dug into her spaghetti and twirled up the last few strands. Winning the fashion contest was a dream come true, she thought blissfully. But when she looked at it from another angle, she decided it was destined to happen all along. After all, she *was* the obvious choice.

"Honestly." Alice Wakefield shook her head in amazement. "I can't understand why a pretty girl like that would have to be so sneaky."

Across the dinner table, Jessica met her twin's eyes and made a sour grimace. "Pretty girl," she muttered darkly. "Humph." That wasn't the expression she would have picked to describe Pamela Janson.

"I'm just glad Lila and Amy pulled the curtain back," Elizabeth pointed out. "That's the smartest thing they've ever done. You should have seen what you looked like, Jess."

Smiling, Jessica nodded and made a mental note to do something special for her friends.

"So when do you get the new clothes?" her mother asked.

Jessica swallowed, then put down her fork. "In a few weeks—Nadine said she'll get back to me. She has to go to Italy for a show," she added in a wistful tone.

"She should have taken you with her," Ned Wakefield said. "The new Nadine model." He gave her a wink.

Jessica brightened. "Maybe I should try modeling again."

"Forget it." Mrs. Wakefield cut her off, laughing.

Grinning, Jessica peeked at her mother from under her lashes and gave her a sheepish look. "Just a thought."

"Come on, Jess. Help me clear the table." Elizabeth stood up and gave her twin a look of understanding. Her eyes twinkled with hidden laughter.

Jessica pouted, but she managed an airy shrug. "OK." She followed Elizabeth into the kitchen.

As soon as Elizabeth set down her stack of dishes, she turned on Jessica with an excited grin. "So what did he say?"

"Who?" Jessica replied innocently. She knew her twin was curious to know how A.J. had reacted to the incident, and since there had been so much confusion and hurrying around after the show, they hadn't had a real chance to talk it over.

"Jessica!"

She let out a giggle, and her blue-green eyes sparkled in a way they hadn't in weeks. "Well, let me see if I can remember his exact words," she said with a sigh, leaning against the counter. "First of all, there was 'Congratulations on winning—'"

"*Jessica!*" With a playful punch on Jessica's shoulder, Elizabeth faced her squarely and looked her in the eye. "Was there anything like 'I never realized what a fantastic, wonderful, exciting person you were before today'?" she demanded, folding her arms across her chest. "Or, 'Gee, Jessica. I thought you were so boring before, but wow! You're really great.' "

Jessica lowered her eyes, and a blush of pleasure tinged her cheeks. What A.J. had said to her after the show was going to stay a private memory for a long time. And she would never forget the look in his eyes. It was a look that said things weren't hopeless after all! When she had thought that everything would be decided at the fashion contest, she had been right. She just hadn't expected such a perfect resolution.

"I guess that idea I had was kind of dumb,"

she admitted shyly, shaking her head. "Trying to act that way didn't exactly work the way I thought it would."

Elizabeth groaned. "Didn't I tell you a million times?" she wailed. "You practically drove him out of town!"

"OK, OK! You made your point." Jessica scraped off a dinner plate and rinsed it. Now that she looked back on it, she couldn't understand how she had gotten such a scheme into her head. She cast a sidelong glance at her sister. "And I should've listened to you. Thanks for trying."

"I was worried about you, Jess. I didn't want you to get hurt. And Lila and Amy and Cara were working on you, too, you know."

Jessica laughed cynically. "I noticed."

There was a short pause as the two girls stacked dishes in the dishwasher. Finally Elizabeth broke the silence. "So . . . what are you doing tonight, anyway?" she asked in a casual tone.

"Oh, I think I'll study, maybe write a few poems—ow!" Jessica let out a squawk as her sister poked her in the ribs. Then both of them stopped to listen as the door bell rang at the front of the house.

Elizabeth turned on Jessica with a knowing look. "Expecting somebody?"

Smiling serenely, Jessica shrugged one shoulder. "Hmm. I wonder who that could be?"

"Jessica?" Mrs. Wakefield's voice came in from the front hall. "Jessica! A.J.'s here!"

"Tell him I'll be there in a few minutes!" she called back. Grinning at her twin, she added, "It never hurts to keep 'em waiting."

Thirteen

Jessica and A.J. were walking along the beach, hand in hand, watching the sunset. Being with him now gave Jessica a thrill of exhilaration that she knew came from being in love. She let out a sigh and sent him a warm smile.

"What are you thinking about?" he asked. His brown eyes were dark and sultry in the fading light.

Jessica grinned and kicked her bare feet through the sand. "I was just thinking how you must have thought I was the most boring person on the whole planet."

"Oh, no, I—"

"It's OK." She said, laughing and swinging their hands back and forth. "I would have thought so, too."

He tilted his head to one side and regarded

her thoughtfully. "I don't get it. Why were you doing all those things if you didn't want to?"

"I thought you'd like me," she mumbled.

"What?"

She drew a deep breath and faced him squarely. "I thought you'd like me that way," she confessed. "I didn't think you'd like the way I really am."

A.J. stared at her. "Are you kidding me?"

"No. I mean, I'm usually more like—well, like Pamela, to tell you the truth."

"I don't believe it."

"It's true," she said, letting out a deep sigh. "I do a lot of nasty things." A small wave washed up over their ankles and pulled back again. She peeked up at him through her lashes, waiting to see how he would take it.

"Jessica, maybe you have your own way of doing things, but you're not like her. She has a real mean streak."

"That's true!" Jessica's eyes lingered on A.J.'s face, absorbing every detail. She had never been so happy in her life. "I guess I was acting pretty dumb," she continued. "But I had a good reason."

He grinned at her, and his intense gaze sent shivers up her spine. "What was the reason?"

"Mmm. I'll tell you later," she said slowly.

Their eyes met in the faint sunset glow. Jessica might have gone about getting A.J. in the wrong way, but it had worked out in the end—a thousand times better than she had expected.

"Come on. There's a place I want to show you," she said suddenly, heading toward his car.

"Where?"

"I'm not telling. Just drive where I say."

Her eyes dancing, Jessica directed A.J. away from the beach, through town, and up the road to Miller's Point. Every time he asked where they were going, she stubbornly refused to tell him. At last they pulled up at the overlook, and A.J. cut the engine.

"This is Miller's Point," she explained, her voice earnest and hopeful. "A lot of people come up here at night to see the lights from town."

A.J. was looking at her steadily in the darkness. "Oh, yeah?" he drawled. He moved closer to her and put one arm along the back of her seat. "Lights, huh?"

"That's right," she teased. Her pulse was racing wildly. Trying to keep her voice even, she continued, "See, isn't it a nice view?"

"Very nice."

A.J. reached out and touched Jessica's cheek. It was very still and quiet inside the car, and Jessica could hear her own heartbeat drumming in her ears. "Nice," she murmured, leaning toward him.

Their lips met in a long, lingering kiss. Finally Jessica sat back and gave A.J. a lazy smile. "We should have come here a long time ago," she said in a low, throaty voice.

He chuckled softly and nodded. "If you'd kissed me like that before, we could have been doing something else besides watching birds for the past couple of weeks."

Jessica laughed and put her arms around his neck. "Well, there aren't any birds here now," she whispered. "Let's not waste any more time."

Elizabeth and Enid walked into the lunchroom on Monday and found a crowd of their friends sitting together at a big table. "Any room for us?" Elizabeth asked, giving the group a lopsided smile.

"No, no! Go away," Winston growled. He was reading the new edition of *The Oracle*, which had come out that morning.

Jeffrey tossed a balled-up lunch bag at Winston and nodded to two chairs. "Come on."

"Thanks."

"Everyone's talking about Jessica winning the fashion contest," Sandra Bacon informed them. "It's so fantastic."

"Yeah, she's really excited about it," Elizabeth agreed. She glanced across the cafeteria to where her twin was seated next to A.J. at an isolated table. From the looks of things, Jessica was more excited about winning A.J. than anything else. Their heads were close together, and they were deep in conversation. As Elizabeth watched, Jessica let out a peal of laughter and shook her head.

Smiling to herself, Elizabeth reached for a copy of the newspaper and snapped it open. Usually she read all the articles before the paper went to press, but she liked to see the final edition. She always turned to her own column first.

Quickly scanning the "Eyes and Ears" column, Elizabeth kept half her attention on the conversation around her. A voice caught her ear.

"Who's J.W.?" Cara asked. "Hey, Liz?"

She looked up. "Yes?"

"In your column you say, 'Will J.W., rumored to be Sweet Valley's best ballerina, try out for the dance lead?' " Cara looked puzzled. "I know it's not Jessica, so who's J.W.?"

"Jade Wu," Elizabeth explained. "Olivia told me she's probably the best dancer we've got. But I've never seen her dance, and I don't know if she's even interested in auditioning."

Cara nodded thoughtfully and then shrugged. "Well, I guess we'll know this week at the tryouts."

"Right." Elizabeth glanced around the cafeteria, her curiosity piqued. She didn't know anything about Jade, but she trusted Olivia's judgment. If Olivia said Jade was talented, then Elizabeth believed her. Unconsciously she searched the crowd for a glimpse of the girl. Finally she spotted her in a corner, bent over a copy of *The Oracle*. Jade looked concerned—almost troubled.

Shrugging, Elizabeth went back to her lunch. They'd know soon enough if Jade Wu was going to audition for the show.

On the other side of the cafeteria, Jade Wu reread the "Eyes and Ears" column for the third time. "Will J.W., rumored to be Sweet Valley's best ballerina, try out for the dance lead? Stay tuned, folks. The auditions are this week."

Feeling slightly sick, Jade realized she *had* to be the one the column was talking about. She didn't know how Elizabeth Wakefield could know about her dancing, but it didn't matter now. What mattered was trying out for the show.

I have to get a part, she told herself fervently. *Being a dancer means dancing in public*.

She pictured herself pirouetting across a stage in a blaze of lights. But instantly that picture was replaced by one of her father. Traditional and conservative, her father would never agree to let her perform in a variety show. She was sure of it.

He's so Chinese, she thought. *It's not fair! Doesn't he realize that I'm American? Doesn't he know this isn't the old country?*

Straightening her back, Jade folded the paper and nodded decisively. She was going to get that part, no matter what her father said.

Will Jade Wu win the leading dance role in the variety show? Find out in Sweet Valley High #50, **OUT OF REACH**.

YOUR OWN

SWEET VALLEY HIGH®

SLAM BOOK!

If you've read *Slambook Fever*, Sweet Valley High #48, you know that slam books are the rage at Sweet Valley High. Now *you* can have a slam book of your own! Make up your own categories, such as "Biggest Jock" or "Best Looking," and have your friends fill in the rest! There's a four-page calendar, horoscopes and questions most asked by Sweet Valley readers with answers from Elizabeth and Jessica

Watch for FRANCINE PASCAL'S SWEET VALLEY HIGH SLAM BOOK, on sale in September. It's a must for SWEET VALLEY fans!

SUPER THRILLERS

☐ **26905 DOUBLE JEOPARDY #1**　　　　**$2.95**

When the twins get part-time jobs on the Sweet Valley newspaper, they're in for some chilling turn of events. The "scoops" Jessica invents to impress a college reporter turn into the real thing when she witnesses an actual crime—but now no one will believe her! The criminal has seen her car, and now he's going after Elizabeth. The twins have faced danger and adventure before ... but never like this!

☐ **27230 ON THE RUN #2**　　　　**$2.95**

Elizabeth is attracted to Eric Hankman who is working with the twins at the newspaper. Eric feels the same, but he's very secretive. When the truth comes out— Eric's father testified against a mob leader and was given a new identity under a witness protection program—it leads to a deadly confrontation for Eric and Elizabeth!

EXCITING NEWS FOR ROMANCE READERS

Loveletters—the all new, hot-off-the-press Romance Newsletter. Now you can be the first to know:

What's Coming Up:
* Exciting offers
* New romance series on the way

What's Going Down:
* The latest gossip about the SWEET VALLEY HIGH gang
* Who's in love . . . and who's not
* What Loveletters fans are saying.

Who's New:
* Be on the inside track for upcoming titles

If you don't already receive Loveletters, fill out this coupon, mail it in, and you will receive Loveletters several times a year. Loveletters . . . you're going to love it!

Please send me my free copy of Loveletters

Name _____ Date of Birth _____

Address _____

City _____ State _____ Zip _____

To: LOVELETTERS
    BANTAM BOOKS
    PO BOX 1005
    SOUTH HOLLAND, IL 60473

SD6—10/88

SWEET VALLEY HIGH

Prices and availability subject to change without notice

Buy them at your local bookstore or use this page to order.

- -

Bantam Books, Dept. SVH2, 414 East Golf Road, Des Plaines, IL 60016

Please send me the books I have checked above. I am enclosing $_____
(please add $2.00 to cover postage and handling). Send check or money order
—no cash or C.O.D.s please.

Mr/Ms _____

Address _____

City/State _____ Zip _____

SVH2—8/88

Please allow four to six weeks for delivery. This offer expires 2/89.

Special Offer
Buy a Bantam Book
for only 50¢.

Now you can order the exciting books you've been wanting to read straight from Bantam's latest catalog of hundreds of titles. *And* this special offer gives you the opportunity to purchase a Bantam book for only 50¢. Here's how:

By ordering any five books at the regular price per order, you can also choose any other single book listed (up to a $5.95 value) for only 50¢. Some restrictions do apply, so for further details send for Bantam's catalog of titles today.

Just send us your name and address and we'll send you Bantam Book's SHOP AT HOME CATALOG!